Viviane Moore was
where her father w
stained-glass artist.
and worked as a jo
group. Her main are of
the Middle Ages and for some time she has devoted
herself full-time to writing her novels featuring
the Chevalier Galeran de Lesneven. She lives in La
Rochelle in France. *The Darkest Red* is the third
'Galeran' mystery.

THE DARKEST RED

Viviane Moore

Translated by
Adriana Hunter

ORION

An Orion paperback

First published in Great Britain in 2001
by Orion
This paperback edition published in 2002
by Orion Books Ltd,
Orion House, 5 Upper St Martin's Lane,
London WC2H 9EA

A CIP catalogue record for this book
is available from the British Library.

ISBN 0 75284 475 X

Printed and bound in Great Britain by
Clays Ltd, St Ives plc

THE DARKEST RED

The Abbey of Jumièges
in the 12th Century

1 Church of Notre~Dame
2 Church of Saint~Pierre
3 Storeroom
4 Kitchens
5 Cloister
6 Chapter House
7 Reliquary Room
8 Library
9 Scriptorium
10 Dorter
11 Frater House
12 Ovens
13 Bath House
14 Hostelry
15 Vegetable
    Garden
16 Medicinal
    Garden
17 Orchard
18 Stables
19 Gate House
20 Stock Yard
21 Herbarium

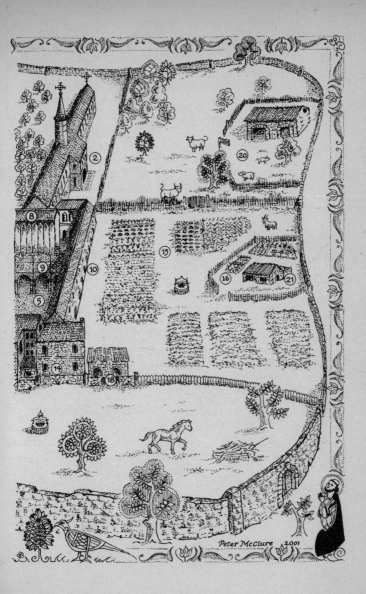

Peter McClure 2001

Prologue

'The Leviathan maketh the deep to boil like a pot:
   He maketh a path to shine after him.'

Book of Job

The great equinox tide was drawing near. For several days now a terrible storm had been raging over the Normandy coast. The shoreline was frozen by the northerly winds. The furious waves billowed up into the estuaries, struck out at the cliffs, and flooded the drainage ditches and the low-lying plains.

The seagulls silently veered inland in their thousands. Schools of fish, seals and blower whales left the high seas and swarmed back to the still warm waters of the shore and the mouth of the Seine . . .

On that September morning of 1145, in a spell of bright weather, two watchmen morosely contemplating the glittering expanse of the river suddenly saw a column of white vapour rising from the water and falling back down in fine oily droplets . . .

An enormous whale had just surfaced up-river from Caudebec.

'*Baloena! Baloena!*' The watchmen's strident cries were soon answered by the hoarse blaring of the horns which spread out for miles over the forest and all the way to Jumièges Abbey where the bells began to swing, calling the monks and peasants to put down their work and run over to the great river.

The whale was slowly making its way up the course of the Seine. It stayed at the surface, and its black outline encrusted with barnacles looked like an island drifting over the troubled waters with a cortège of white birds.

The river suddenly seemed sorely narrow for this giant of the cold seas. Nevertheless, the ancient chronicles bore testimony to the fact that in days gone by the monks at Jumièges had seen marine monsters as vast as the towers of their own abbey. For several years now, however, the whales had been more scarce. They had become wary, as if the calls of the watchmen warned them of the terrible fate that was to befall them.

They stayed out at sea and no longer allowed themselves to be seduced by the treacherous calm of the rivers. Only the terrible equinoctial tides and the most powerful of storms drove them inland.

At Jumièges, men, women, the young and the old were all running towards the little port. Here and there in the river, the peasants were securing the last parts of the three great nets that were to stop the creature at the foot of the Abbey of Saint Philibert.

Terrified by the approach of the great blower whale, the women of the village tried to keep their youngest close to them. Those children who escaped their mothers' clutches were already perched up in trees or on the roofs, trying to get a glimpse of this Leviathan as it approached their homes.

Suddenly the crowd parted, cleaving a path for a young Nordic god whose great stature and fair colouring betrayed his origins.

'Rurik, it is Rurik the Dane,' whispered the villagers.

Without appearing to notice the excitement that he generated, the young man came up to the bank and studied the river carefully. Rurik, wearing a sturdy rope around his naked torso and armed with slender lances, was charged with putting the Leviathan to death. The abbey paid him to do so.

The last echoes of the bell had fallen quiet and a great silence spread through the crowd which stood hard up along the bank.

The whale was coming closer, it would soon be beyond Yainville.

'Hvalt!' exclaimed Rurik, indicating the Beast's dark outline. 'May God preserve us!'

The monks crossed themselves, women fell to their knees in fear, hiding their heads in their hands. Instinctively, the men clenched their fists, estimating the size of the animal: it was larger than their own cottages.

A signal from downstream announced that the fishermen had closed off the trap and set the nets which would stop the whale from escaping back to the open sea.

The Leviathan was caught in the trap. The chase was about to begin.

Monks with their habits lifted up and knotted to their belts, and with water half-way up their calves, helped the peasants to push their long boats into the river.

Each boat contained motley piles of bows, lances, grappling hooks and hefty logs of wood. The men were already taking up their oars and pulling hard on them to get into the middle of the Seine.

The whale was till ploughing forward, and the grey marbling along it black spine could now be seen close to the bank where the villagers were standing.

The young Dane had leapt into a light boat which he man-oeuvred with surprising speed, drawing level with the villagers' heavier craft in the twinkling of an eye.

He overtook them effortlessly and slid his vessel to within a few feet of the great blower. The seagulls described wide circles overhead. The men were now standing in their boats, aiming their lances and their bows, waiting for the signal from the Dane.

The whale had come to a halt. It had sensed man. Rurik chose this moment to fire his weapon. The Dane knew that he had to touch that point at the very top of the monster's back that his ancestors had called its 'life'. He steadied the lance in his hand and threw it with great force.

The weapon ripped through the air and quivered as it pierced into the whale's flesh, missing its target by a good foot but injuring the animal in the lung.

Rurik rushed to his oars. A spray of foam made him look up and he just had time to see the vast shadow of the whale's tail coming between him and the sun.

Soaked and straining forward with the exertion, the Dane just managed to slip his boat clear as the mighty tail fell back onto the surface of the water.

Pierced by the spear and reeling from the pain, the whale spun round on itself, creating towering waves that crashed violently onto the shores, scattering the curious onlookers.

With the point still planted in its flesh, the monster sped ahead through the waters of the river before throwing itself into the first row of nets, tearing them to shreds.

Standing up on his vessel, Rurik yelled out an order, and the fishermen let off a volley of arrows which stuck into the beast's dark spine. The men hastily threw the logs overboard to hamper the giant's progress.

Covered in wounds and streaming with blood, the whale abandoned the nets and turned round once again to face the boats. It remained motionless and blew a long jet of water tinged with pink. The men waited, a powerful, spicy scent enveloping them. The air suddenly seemed colder.

Then the Leviathan charged, forging straight towards its captors, a huge black bulk, as tall as a hill, capsizing everything in its path, indiscriminately crushing boats and sawn logs.

Screams of terror and pain sprang from the shattered craft. Most of the men could not swim. In their fear they lost their reason, clung to each other in panic and sank to the bottom together.

Rurik, who had managed to steer clear hastily, stood up in his boat, holding a spear with a gleaming point in his hand.

Rocked by the waves, the young man took a moment to balance himself and then, as if aiming at the sun, he straightened his arm up into the sky. Whistling through the air, the iron point made a wide curve before driving fatally into the whale.

The Dane let out a shout of triumph, which was quickly silenced by the terrible upheaval which whisked up his boat and hurled it violently into the river.

The whale, still trying to get back to the open sea, continued to bear straight ahead, a plume of crimson vapour spewing from its blowhole. A huge dark red stain was spreading over the troubled waters of the river. The seagulls described one last circle and flew off, calling mournfully.

Rurik, who had managed to cling to a log, crossed himself. He had won, the whale was 'flowering' dark crimson blooms into the sky. Soon it would be dead.

A few moments later, the whale pitched and rolled, raising a flipper to the sky before exposing its pallid belly.

PART ONE

'Walk while ye have the light,
lest darkness come upon you:
for he that walketh in darkness
knoweth not whither he goeth.'

Gospel according to St John, 12 XXXV

1

'Sit down, my son. I was expecting you.'

With these words, Arnulphe, Bishop of Lisieux, greeted Galeran de Lesneven, and thus began one of the young chevalier's strangest investigations.

Galeran made a tall and imposing silhouette; he threw his brown mantle over his shoulder and bent respectfully before the man of God. 'I thank you, Your Grace, but I will remain standing. I did not know that Bernard de Clairvaux had informed you of my visit other than by this parchment,' he said, taking a rolled, sealed vellum from his purse and handing it to the Bishop.

Arnulphe took the manuscript without replying and read the elegant calligraphy of the Abbot of Clairvaux, surreptitiously watching the young chevalier all the while. Eventually, he nodded several times and put the parchment down.

'Are you from Brittany, my Lord Galeran?'

The young chevalier's blue eyes looked steadily at the Bishop before he replied, 'From Léon on my father's side, and Gascony on my mother's, Your Grace. And knight errant of my own volition,' he added simply.

'Bernard de Clairvaux seems to think very highly of you.'

'He does me great honour, Your Grace.'

'He tells me in this letter that you are a man of great reading and that my library, or should I say the library in my care, would be a delight to you . . .'

'It is so, Your Grace. He mentioned some of the works that you have here, most notably a magnificent copy of Plato's *Timaeus*.'

'He informed you well, my son,' rejoined the Bishop. 'But what a strange desire, for a young chevalier held in such high regard by the court of King Louis, to choose to withdraw into solitude and away from the events of this century.'

'My reputation is not as widespread as you would have it, Your Grace, and I am not truthfully withdrawing. Only, it was God's wish that Bernard de Clairvaux should speak to me of you at a time when I had the misfortune of wanting to forget the death and the damnation of someone with whom I was connected and whom I held dear.'

The chevalier fell silent. The deep scar that ran across his forehead furrowed in response to secret suffering. A heavy silence descended on the audience room in the Bishop's palace. As the chevalier stood waiting in the middle of the vast panelled hall, he thought to himself that the Bishop had a very singular way of receiving visitors. An inquisitive stare filtered beneath the Bishop's heavy eyelids.

Galeran apparently came through this scrutiny successfully, and a subtle smile suddenly drew out the corners of the Bishop's thin mouth. He crossed himself before announcing: 'You are most welcome in my house, Galeran de Lesneven, and may God watch over you and your family.'

The interview had come to an end. A young novice showed the chevalier the cell which had been reserved for him, and his place in the frater. As for Quolibet, Galeran's faithful charger, he was installed in the well-appointed stables of the Bishop's palace, and did not appear to complain about his good fortune.

September 1145, and the acrid smell of the seasonal tide was carried inland by violent winds from the nearby coast. Galeran had cut himself off from the world more than two weeks previously, forgetting his tumultuous life as a knight errant, living as a guest in the Bishop's palace, observing the services and offices with the silent monks, studying in his cell and taking all his meals in the frater with the monks.

He had gradually come to know the strength of the Bishop's personality. His Grace Arnulphe had little more than contempt for the prelates with their gold-trimmed robes, and when high-ranking church dignitaries attended his services he liked to conduct Mass barefoot and in his simplest robes, regardless of whether this pleased or displeased his guests. He was nothing less than the legate of Pope Eugene III, and acted as intermediary between the kingdoms of France and England and the

Duchy of Normandy, where the war between the Empress Maud and King Stephen was creating tension. This did not, however, hamper him from living with the simplicity of a hermit.

During an audience he was once seen to accept gifts from a rich lord whose depraved habits were widely known, only to drop them scornfully to the ground. The Bishop was heard to exclaim in front of the gathered assembly that he had no use for flasks and vessels encrusted with jewels. He would prefer the rich man to do penance in public rather than offering him such gifts.

Such was Arnulphe's character, hard and keen as a blade, and the chevalier began to see what common ground there might be between his Grace and Bernard de Clairvaux.

As the time passed, Bishop Arnulphe grew in friendship towards the chevalier and he would sometimes come to visit him late into the night to talk to him, discussing the works of Abelard just as easily as those of Honorius d'Autun. Galeran took great pleasure in these nocturnal conversations and in his host's profound perception.

One evening, as the meridian of the night approached and Arnulphe was about to leave the chevalier to his manuscripts, he turned at the threshold of the cell and asked: 'Do you know Jumièges, Lord Galeran?'

'Only by name, Your Grace.'

'It is one of the most beautiful abbeys in the Duchy of Normandy, along with Saint-Wandrille and Bec-Hellouin, but that is not why I mentioned it. Jumièges has in its ownership some unique books, and its scriptorium is numbered amongst the best in France and England. There are works there the like of which you will find nowhere else . . .'

Then Arnulphe closed the door, leaving the chevalier a little surprised at his parting words.

But Galeran de Lesneven was to find that the good Bishop never left anything to fate. That the least word from this prince of the Church was calculated, and that he had, without any doubt, been planning his arrival in Normandy and a visit to the sacred abbey of the Terre Gémétique for some time.

2

A few more days passed in study and meditation, until at last the chevalier felt that the time had come for him to take to the road again and return to the kingdom of France. Remembering the Bishop's words, he decided to make a detour to Jumièges. When he informed Arnulphe of his intention, the latter asked whether he would have the grace to come and see him the day before his departure. This he did.

'This way, Chevalier, this way,' said the young novice who was guiding him through the vast halls of the Bishop's palace.

The two men were in the part of the building that was reserved for monks. A long corridor lit by several torches led them past a communal dorter and on to the prelates' cells.

The novice rapped on one of the oak doors, and then hurried away.

'Come in, come in, Lord Galeran,' came Arnulphe's voice.

The chevalier went into the Bishop's cell, a favour accorded to none but a select few.

As prescribed by Saint Benoît, the room was extremely simple. It was furnished with just a matting bed, a *tabula plicata* covered with a wad of parchment and two chairs. A richly illuminated copy of the Book of Job lay open on a lectern.

Arnulphe stood at the mullioned window. He turned slowly towards the chevalier and gestured for him to sit down.

'Thank you for coming to see me, Chevalier.'

'I would have come anyway, Your Grace, to thank you – as is my duty – for your hospitality.'

'Do you know the name of Guillaume de Jumièges, my Lord?' asked the Bishop after a brief silence.

'I believe I do, Your Grace. Was he not the worthy monk who in the last century wrote the venerated *De ducibus Normanniae* devoted to the history of the first dukes of Normandy?'

'Precisely, and you could see it, for that manuscript is part of the collection at the library of Jumièges, along with a copy of the Gospels covered in gold leaf and precious stones, which was offered by the monk Renauld at the time of William the Conqueror.'

Arnulphe paused deliberately, seeing what effect his words had had on the chevalier, and then continued.

'I have written a brief for the attention of Eustache, the Abbot of Jumièges, asking that he might allow you to circulate freely within the abbey and give you access to the scriptorium, the archives and the reliquary.'

'My thanks to you, Your Grace, for your kindness and the care you have taken on my behalf.'

'May I ask you a favour in return?' asked the Bishop abruptly.

'I am your servant, Your Grace.'

'Well, it so happens that I am delegating one of my prelates to Jumièges, and would like it if you were to travel together if, of course, you have no objection.'

'As it please you. It would not displease me to have a travelling companion to while away the journey, and I promise to merit the trust you are placing in me.'

'I am sure you will, my Lord, and it is for that very reason that I would like you to ensure his safety, even once he is within the confines of Jumièges.'

'Is this prelate a relation of yours, Your Grace?'

'Why no, but he is dear to me. There are few like him in my bishopric.'

'Naturally, I understand your concern for him during the journey, Your Grace, but it strikes me as unusual to look out for the safety of one of your monks within the very walls of one of your abbeys,' said the chevalier gravely. 'What do you think there is for him to fear there?'

'Oh nothing, my Lord, probably nothing,' said the Bishop evasively, gesturing vaguely with his hand as if he were shooing away an insect. 'Might I introduce him to you? He is in the next door cell.'

The Bishop clapped his hands together and the door opened to reveal the man who was to become Galeran's travelling companion and friend, Brother Odon of Lisieux.

He had a smooth face with a short ruddy beard, and a small,

rotund body. He seemed to look on the world with indulgence, and the world had apparently looked on him in the same way.

At first glance, one might easily think that Odon was barely more than twenty years old and that he was something of a dreamer. And yet there burned in his little brown eyes a disconcerting blend of humour and assurance. He greeted the chevalier, holding his hand in his for a while and, in that moment, the chevalier understood by the warmth of his grasp and the candour of his expression why Arnulphe might care for this man as he would for a son.

3

Leaving Lisieux at dawn the next day, the two mounted travellers took an ancient Roman road towards the Abbey of Le Bec Hellouin and then, stopping to ask their way several times, cut across the woods and made their way towards the Seine.

Having spent his early childhood looking after horses, Brother Odon rode well and even seemed to take some pleasure in it, using his heels and his voice to guide his mount – one of the Bishop's mares, a beautiful creature with a glossy coat and a powerful outline.

The same could not be said for the novice who accompanied them. The young Ansegise had never ridden before and perched lopsidedly on a plodding mule, panicking each time the animal strayed from the path or seemed unwilling to go on.

Having noticed these shortcomings, Odon had taken the pack mule by the halter, and the little band continued peacefully on their way. Galeran thought that, at this pace, they would not reach Jumièges until late morning.

He rode in front, thinking all the while of the Bishop's recommendations as he struggled to control his charger's bursts of energy. After long days of inactivity in the stables of the Bishop's palace, the valiant Quolibet needed to stretch his legs, and Galeran allowed him to canter on from time to time before turning back and joining his companions.

Asking the way from a little girl taking her goats to pasture, the three riders set off on a path that crossed a magnificent beech grove. The trunks of the ancient trees were clad in grey moss, and tall ferns curved just under the horses' chests. The pathway was covered with weeds and pale blue wild flowers. According to the girl, they were not far from the great river now. Even though it was windy, as was often the case at the time of the equinox, it was a beautiful day. The sun shone down through the high branches and Galeran began to whistle an old regional tune.

4

Abruptly the three riders came to a halt. Everything was quiet but an unbearable smell hung in the morning air: a terrible stench of death, like a charnel house or a battlefield.

Galeran's gelding whinnied nervously, his upper lip curled back, and the chevalier saw tall plumes of black smoke through a gap in the trees. His hand went to his quillon and he gestured with it for his companions to join him. The woods seemed suddenly uncommonly quiet and something mysterious, troubling, hovered behind the dark column of smoke, billows of which were blown back by the wind and wound their way towards the riders, stinging their eyes and noses.

'I have never smelt anything like it, what is this smell, Chevalier, is it a funeral pyre?' asked Odon anxiously.

'I know not, but I like it even less. It is like the smell of burning bones and flesh. Stay close to me from now on, and the novice too.'

The cart track went on down to the Seine, but they still could not see the river which was hidden by the high branches and the thickets. Then suddenly, coming round a sharp bend, they emerged onto an esplanade of closely cropped grass. They were dazzled by a great light, and stopped in amazement.

The wide meanders of the river unfurled at their feet and the Abbey of Jumièges rose luminous and clear on the opposite bank. Jumièges the Alms-giver dominating the forest like a figurehead with its tall towers.

When they saw at last what lay on the bank, the three men understood the origin of the terrible smell that rose up to greet them.

With its immense tail still floating in the current, the bloody carcass of a whale was run aground on the beach. A crowd of men, women and children swirled around the gigantic corpse, like a swarm of flies on carrion. The black smoke they had seen from the path came from constructions of brick that formed a circle around the monster's remains.

'What on earth is that fish the size of a ship?' asked Odon who had not seen a great blower before.

'A whale,' replied Galeran, smiling at the monk's astonishment. 'I have often seen them beached in my country, but I did not know that they came so far inland.'

'But what are all these people doing? Are they burning it?'

'I know not, Brother Odon. Come on, let's go. Look, the abbey's ferry is coming across,' said Galeran pointing to a large raft leaving the port of Jumièges and making for the opposite bank. The chevalier gave his charger a kick and it launched itself at the slope, followed by the little band.

Knight, novice and monk soon arrived on a gently sloping part of the bank, edged with reeds. There were nets and creels drying on the thick grass. A few gloomy-faced labourers from the neighbouring hamlets were waiting for the ferry, weighed down with baskets. They made way for the chevalier and his companions, and greeted them with a brief nod of their heads. Having negotiated their crossing with the ferryman, Galeran led the horses onto the wide old raft, and it slid slowly along its ropes towards the other bank of the Seine and the port of Jumièges.

During the short crossing, the passengers were amazed to see great areas of swamp in various parts of the river, protected by the ramparts of chalk cliffs. Here and there water lilies displayed their cup-shaped flowers, and woodcocks flew off into the reeds, crying in alarm. Fish leapt out of the water round the ferry. Despite the stench unleashed by the enormous black corpse and the ovens, everything seemed peaceful. And yet, the closer the ferry came to Jumièges, the greater the chevalier's feeling of foreboding grew.

He knitted his brows when he saw two old fishermen crossing themselves before lighting a large fire made of damaged fishing boats. The flames flew up quickly, tall and transparent, instantly consuming the wood, devouring the hulls with the naïve drawings on their prows, as the old men looked on.

The ferry thudded against the bank and the three men waited for the labourers to alight before leading off their horses.

The port of Jumièges consisted of numerous little cabins built of loosely joined planks of wood. Everything seemed to be here only temporarily, even the boats which did not stay in the water but were hauled up with pulleys to the village that lay half-way up to the abbey, behind high embankments.

A wide stony road, flanked by a few low-slung houses, led to the great door of the abbey. Everything was built here on the hill, as close as possible to the walls of Jumièges. It was as if the inhabitants were afraid of being invaded from the river, as in the days of the Vikings with their long ships with dragons' heads.

'Shall we go and greet my brother the Abbot straight away, Chevalier?' asked Brother Odon, coughing in the acrid smoke.

'Not yet, Brother. I'd like to observe what's going on here a little more closely. It is rare for fishermen to burn their boats. Even damaged ones; they always try to repair them.'

'Unless they are connected with something evil,' muttered Odon, crossing himself.

Galeran turned to the monk: 'That is what I was thinking, and I would like to know exactly what sort of evil this is. Ansegise!' he called loudly.

The young novice, who had been gazing dreamily at the sky, jumped and blushed as if he had been caught doing wrong.

'Yes, my Lord?'

'You will watch our steeds. Tie them up to that copse over there, and make sure that no one – no one, do you hear me – comes close to them.'

'Of course, my Lord, I'll make sure.'

'Well, Odon. If we want to see what this is all about . . . As I'm responsible for your life with my own, I will not leave your side.'

Odon followed on Galeran's heels and announced humorously: 'Nor will I leave yours, Chevalier, if I am to be guarded more closely than a treasured relic . . .'

The chevalier put his hand on the little monk's shoulder and asked steadily, 'Odon, until now I have not asked you any questions, but I would all the same like to know whether you think you genuinely have something to fear in coming here.'

'Why no, my Lord, my mission within the sacred abbey is a simple one,' replied Odon, looking up at him.

'Arnulphe did not see fit to inform me of the object of your

19

journey,' continued the chevalier. 'I simply thought that you had been appointed here, and that is obviously not the case. Have you been sent here by the bishopric of Lisieux?'

'Oh, I can assure you, my Lord, that it is nothing to worry about, religious matters, nothing more. I do not know why the Bishop is being so careful. But then, he asked me not to disclose anything, so . . .'

'So, we will respect his wishes,' the chevalier agreed simply.

As they spoke, the two men drew closer to the body of the Leviathan. It seemed that the whole village along with the inhabitants of the neighbouring hamlets, as well as the monks from the abbey, had convened to cut up the beast.

Some fifteen men toiled over it, cutting strips of meat and fat with long-handled knives.

Children, scurrying backwards and forwards, climbed up ladders onto the whale's back and heaved buckets full of fat over to the monks, who cut the pieces up before throwing them into the great melting pots. Between the corpse, which had begun decomposing rapidly overnight, and the nauseating smell of the burning fat, the stench was intolerable. But the villagers did not seem to notice it, busy as they were cutting, slicing, salting and curing all the flesh. Even though they risked scalding themselves, children dunked hunks of bread into the melting pots and scampered off delighted with their booty, devouring it avidly.

The chevalier, who had never beheld such a process, came up to the constructions of brick that surrounded the animal.

'Hail to you, Chevalier,' said a little old man with a tanned face who came up to the young man, limping. 'You be not from these parts.'

'Why no, my good man, I'm from Léon.'

'Where's that, then?'

'At the ends of the earth, my friend.'

'That'll be far, then,' whistled the old man admiringly. 'I'm the one they call the Sven, but I'm too old to help, and then the old legs don't work so good, so I just chat to folk.'

'My name is Galeran de Lesneven. But tell me, what is it you are doing here?' asked the chevalier, indicating the bulbous cauldrons.

'Oh, that, it is for the oil, for Jumièges. The monks use it to light their way in winter. You have to keep a big fire going beneath it,' said the old man, showing them the blazing fire. 'And you put the beast's fat to melt in there. And this,' he said pointing to some tall vats, 'is water as cold as winter ice. You pour the oil onto it and leave it to rest. Then all the muck drops to the bottom, and you just have to put it into barrels and load it onto the carts. I have done this plenty of times, I can tell you. We had no end of whales when I was a lad, and the whole place would celebrate. Just think! There was plenty to eat for months to come, for us and the monks too. But things are not so happy now, there's some as have died. It's all Rurik's fault. Shouldn't hunt with him, you shouldn't, brings bad luck, he does.'

The chevalier leapt at his words.

'Died? You mean some men from the village died chasing this as game? Did it not beach itself?'

'Oh, you should have seen it,' continued the old man without paying any attention to the chevalier's words. 'It is all Rurik really. Us, we just do as we're told. Him, he knows what to do with those lances, have to know what you're doing. He's the one as killed it. Look, that's him over there, the tall one that looks like a Dane!' muttered the old boy.

A young, blond giant was standing over by a thicket of trees. He was looking at the ovens and his pale eyes rested for a moment on those of the chevalier. Then he turned away and disappeared into the trees.

'Thank you, the Sven, and may God keep you,' answered the chevalier, looking round for Odon.

He had just been talking to one of the monks and was standing motionless in front of the whale, looking up at it as he might have done at a cathedral.

'So, Odon, what do you think of it?'

Odon was staring at the massive jaws bristling with baleen that the fishermen were pulling out systematically.

'It is strange, I would never have imagined Jonah's whale like this . . .'

'You're right, Odon, it is indeed a strange animal, and there is some sadness in seeing it in this state. The tales of its travels across the seas would fill several volumes.'

The monk nodded thoughtfully.

'You managed to talk to one of the abbey's monks . . . what did he tell you?' probed the chevalier.

'Well, this whale did not die on its own, they hunted it. Men actually killed such a Leviathan, Galeran!' said Odon, indicating the massive bulk whose flesh was being carved up to dissolve in the blackened cauldrons.

'Yes, and I admit that I cannot really imagine such a hunt. I'd heard that the Basques of Biscay killed whales in their hundreds, but I thought those were fables for infants. The old Sven told me that some have lost their lives . . .'

'It is a strange story. The abbey should be able to rejoice over what it has gained from this hunt, but the monks have lost one of their number.'

'Do you mean to say that the monks join in the hunt with the villagers?'

'Why no. The hunt did not go well yesterday, the fishermen were not as speedy as the Dane who was in charge of them and who, incidentally, is paid by the Abbot Eustache for such service. Two boats full of men capsized. They managed to save several of them and to fish out some bodies, but this morning they found more washed up onto the swamp including one body which had no business there, because it was the body of a monk.'

'A monk,' repeated the chevalier.

'Yes, the Under-Sexton from Jumièges, Brother Joce.'

The chevalier nodded thoughtfully as he watched the women heaving chunks of meat over to some tables where the old women salted them before tossing them into barrels.

The miraculous fishing expedition would feed the village and light the abbey for many a long month. And yet the spectre of death hovered overhead, leaving its cold grey mask on the faces of these villagers who had lost several of their number in one blow.

5

'Upon my beard, look, Galeran! They've left the bodies on the river bank. The monk told me that they were going to hold a solemn mass this evening, but I hadn't realised that they'd abandoned these unfortunate souls like this. It goes against all the rules.'

Odon pointed to where, a few feet from them, six bodies lay barely covered by sheets of canvas. There was something sinister about these vulnerable remains lying in the very shadow of the Leviathan that had killed them.

The two men approached slowly. The chevalier was the first to lean over a shroud, which he lifted to reveal the blueish face of a fisherman whose eyes, bulging with water, protruded from their sockets. A fine white foam trickled from his mouth and nostrils, indicating a massive inhalation of water. The poor man's naked arms and legs were covered with bruises.

Galeran put the sheet back down and went on to the second shroud. Eventually he stopped to throw back the sheet that covered the body of the under-sexton of Jumièges, and he knelt to examine it more closely. The unfortunate monk's face was pallid and his eyes too bulged from their sockets.

'What is it that you're looking for?' asked Brother Odon uneasily.

'To see whether this monk really did drown, Brother,' replied the chevalier, briefly, as he examined the body's hands with its bitten fingernails.

Odon made a gesture of surprise but, seeing that he would get nothing more out of Galeran, he moved some distance away and knelt to pray for the eternal rest of these poor drowned souls.

The chevalier gently turned the head of the corpse and confirmed that his neck was not broken. Then he looked closely at the fine scratch marks on both sides of the neck before covering the body up again and getting to his feet, a thoughtful expression on his face.

'Who are you and who gave you permission to touch the bodies?' barked a voice behind him.

Galeran turned round slowly and looked intently at his questioner before replying. The man, a churchman with an imposing physique and a dry, nervous manner, wore the black robes of the Benedictine order. A heavy gold chain bearing a crucifix hung round his neck.

'My name is Galeran de Lesneven, and I was sent by His Grace Arnulphe, Bishop of Lisieux.'

'A chevalier,' the monk exclaimed in astonishment, 'His Grace is sending us a chevalier now, is he?'

'No, Brother Prior,' said a small calm voice, 'the Bishop of Lisieux actually sent me, Brother Odon. What my Lord Galeran means is that he has come to spend a while in the Terre Gémétique with the blessing of His Grace Arnulphe. And it happens that we travelled here together.'

The prior pursed his lips and asked Odon:

'How do you know who I am?'

'Only he who wrote knows that I am coming, is that not the case?' Odon spoke these enigmatic words with his usual humour, and the Prior sensed that he had gone too far.

'Forgive me such a reception, Brother,' he said, casting his eyes aside, 'I am indeed the Prior, Father Angilbert. This terrible hunt and the death of our poor Brother Joce have devastated me. Please will you excuse me too, Chevalier,' he added turning to Galeran who had followed the exchange attentively.

'For my part, you are quite forgiven, Father,' replied the chevalier. 'We intended to go and greet your superior, Abbot Eustache. Perhaps you could take us to him?'

'Of course, of course, follow me,' the Prior said quietly as he went past them to lead the way.

After going to find Ansegise who was day-dreaming under the shady trees, the three men took their mounts by their halters and slowly climbed the chalk path which led to the abbey.

Father Angilbert walked ahead of them with his habit flying in the wind at each step, and the chevalier thought to himself that it made him look like a crow tossed in a storm.

6

From afar, the monastery had a proud demeanour. A white path led to a vast gateway, which stood open in the long fortified wall.

In honour of the Lord God, the Benedictine monks of Jumièges had built two churches that dominated the roof-line of the towering monastic buildings. One of these churches, a monument as powerful as a cathedral, which was dedicated to Notre-Dame the Virgin Mary, overlooked the monastery with its twin towers topped with spires. The second, a more modest building, was dedicated to the Apostle Peter.

As they drew closer, the two visitors saw that in places there were gaps appearing in the outer wall, where it had been burrowed into by the knotty roots of creeping ivy.

The spires of Notre-Dame had been clumsily repaired, and the rain must surely disturb the serenity of the services from time to time. Even the roofs of the common parts were in a pitiful state. Piles of stone covered in grey moss bore testimony to buildings long since destroyed that had never been rebuilt.

'Your abbey is in a fairly poor state, Brother,' affirmed the chevalier. 'I imagine that these troubled times have not made it easy to make repairs.'

'Indeed, and Jumièges is very old, my Lord, given that it was built by Saint Philibert in 654. At the time, our founding father built a third church dedicated to Saint Denis and Saint Germain, and it has never been restored since. The ancient chronicles relate how Jumièges was pillaged and destroyed by Danish pirates. And, even if that was some three hundred years ago, our community has never succeeded in restoring its former glory. Then, when the war with England raged, our monastery was devastated once again. And now, what with the troubles between the Empress Maud, King Stephen and the Duchy of Normandy! The community is too poor to rebuild its monuments, and our hands too few to accomplish the task, there are no longer enough of us. To think that there were once one hundred and fourteen monks here as well as all those who waited on them!'

Angilbert's bitter voice fell silent and Odon nodded his head:

'*Bene omnia fecit Dominus*, all that the Lord does is good,' he said sententiously. 'How many of you are there in the abbey now, Father?'

'About sixty,' the Prior replied, lowering his eyes. 'And the laymen who work here, as well as a few who have hereditary responsibilties. But most of them live in the hamlet, outside the walls, or at Heurteauville on the other bank.'

'I see. And how many of you officiate here?'

'Um . . . about ten, including the Abbot, Eustache. We're here now. If you will excuse me, I will let Father Abbot know that you have arrived.'

Angilbert moved off without even waiting for a reply.

The porter's lodge was empty, and while they waited to be received by the Abbot, Galeran and Odon decided to have a look round the premises. A huge paved courtyard covered in moss and weeds ran the length of the buildings. Through a porch they could see a vegetable garden divided into regular square plots, cut through by irrigation channels. Beyond, the twisted silhouettes of fruit trees were outlined against the sky.

Near the stables, some servants were hitching up two carriages. They were setting off, on the Abbot's orders, to collect the dead so that they could be prepared for the Mass.

'My Lord, Brothers!' called a voice.

A stable boy came towards them, holding a richly bedecked palfrey by the bridle. The young man was small and dark with a nervous, abrupt manner and a sharp eye. All of his movements betrayed the energy that was contained within him.

'Well, by my faith, that is surely the steed of a prince or a great lord,' exclaimed Galeran. 'Jumièges may well be poor, but its visitors, at least, are not!'

'Quite so, my Lord, but if I had the choice,' said the young man looking closely at Galeran's gelding, 'I would take your charger. He's not so showy, but a war horse with powerful hocks and a good deep chest is worth far more than a creature whose only quality is its beautiful harness or its slender fetlocks.'

'You have a well honed tongue, my friend. Who are you and what do you want?'

'My name is Roderic, my Lord, and I have been sent by the Prior to take charge of your mounts. I must take them to the water trough and then on to the stables with this one.'

'Tell me, whose is this palfrey?'

'He belongs to the son of the Lord of Clères, my Lord Rainolf, who has been staying with us since yesterday with ten of his men.'

Once he had unsaddled the horses and taken the pack off the mule, the young Ansegise followed the groom over to the water trough. An old monk came up to the travellers and indicated a little room where they could wait until someone came to find them. The porter was not there for the moment, he said, and would soon return.

Sitting side by side on a long stone bench, the two men remained silent. Hearing the sound of footsteps, Odon bent quickly towards the chevalier:

'I must leave you, Galeran, Father Abbot will find you a place in the abbey's hostelry, whereas I will go into the communal dorter.'

The chevalier nodded and added quietly, 'I believe I have now guessed your mission, Brother Odon. Look after yourself, there have been "religious visitors" who have come to no good.'

'You have a subtle mind, Galeran, and I am but a lowly dreamer. Who would want any harm to a man like myself?' replied the little monk, hypocritically.

'Your voice betrays the man that you really are, Brother, and the Prior was no dupe. If you do ever dream, it is certainly not when you are working.'

Odon laughed briefly and delivered a friendly thump to the chevalier.

'Look after yourself and I will look after myself, Galeran de Lesneven.'

'Very good,' retorted the chevalier,' but there are things here that do little to please me. Rest assured that I will stay here until you tell me that I can leave without risking any harm to yourself.'

The young monk was moved and he took Galeran's hand, squeezing it briefly in his own.

A Benedictine came over to them and greeted them. He had come for Brother Odon to take him to Father Abbot. Galeran watched Odon's silhouette for a long time as it progressed along the corridor to the abbey. The little monk was bent over as if he were carrying on his shoulders some weight that was too heavy for him.

7

Later, after a brief interview with the Reverend Father Abbot, who received him kindly but apparently had other things on his mind, Galeran followed the Father Hosteller through the abbey's long corridors.

'It is here, Chevalier,' said the Hosteller, opening a small oak door. 'Father Abbot thought that you would like to be alone. The communal room of the hostelry is hardly conducive to study. This cell is used by the Friar Nurse when he prefers to stay close by his patients, otherwise it is used by pilgrims on retreat.'

'It is very well thus, Father, I thank you,' said Galeran.

The Father Hosteller, a tall, strapping, solid-looking man despite his grey hair, seemed in no hurry to leave. With his fan-shaped beard and ironic eye, he was an affable and curious man. The only one with whom pilgrims could speak with impunity, because monastic law did not bind him to silence.

'Oh, but I have not given you my name, I am Father Baudri.'

'And I, Father, am Galeran de Lesneven, chevalier, of Léon.'

'I knew someone who came from those parts, unless he was from Vannetais, I do not really remember . . . The brother in the frater will welcome you if you would like to take your meal with the other pilgrims after Sext Mass. I have arranged for a candle and some fresh water for you. I could take you to the steam room this evening or have a washing basin put at your disposal.'

'The steam room would suit me very well, Father. Being a pilgrim myself, I will take my meals in the frater with the others and will follow the services. I thank you for your help.'

'It is nothing, my son, does not our law tell us to receive passing visitors *tanquam Christus*, as we would Christ himself?'

'May God keep you, Father Baudri, hospitality is not always the norm in these troubled times. Tell me, Father,' asked the young chevalier as he put down his quillon and his saddle, 'did you know the unfortunate Brother Joce well?'

'Um, yes . . . like everyone here,' replied the monk a little hesitantly. 'Even though the Under-Sexton was from the same region as me, a child of Duclair like myself, we hardly saw each other. He had been working for Brother Gachelin for nearly two years now.'

'Gachelin?'

'Yes, our Sexton. Even though Joce did not like him much. God forgive me, but Brother Gachelin is not a barrel of laughs. He was hard on Joce. The poor creature looked after everything here, the hay for the floors, the repairs to the buildings, the bell-ringing . . .'

'Did Brother Joce frequently venture outside the abbey?' asked the chevalier as he took off his heavy travelling mantle and hung it on an iron hook.

'Oh no!' announced the Father Hosteller. 'Even as a child he was nicknamed Joce *le Peor*, Joce the Fear, and as he grew older he was even afraid of his own shadow. To the extent that he would sometimes faint. I really believe that he became a monk to protect himself from the world, poor boy. So, as far as leaving the abbey walls is concerned, that was not his style at all.'

'Many thanks, Father, for this information.'

'At your service, my Lord, and may God keep you,' said the Father Hosteller, leaving the room with obvious regret.

Once the door was closed again, the chevalier took off his ballock dagger and untied his woollen doublet so that he could take off the breastplate that he wore beneath it. This garment of leather and metal seemed incongruous in a place of prayer.

A powerful peppery smell rose up from the foliage that was strewn on the floor. The whitewash on the walls was flaking off, but the straw mattress was thick and gave off a lovely smell of cut hay. The chevalier could not see any evidence of vermin in it. A woollen blanket and a horsehair pillow had been left on a stool. An arrow slit looked out onto the abbey's vegetable garden. In the thin ray of light that filtered through the narrow window Father Baudri had put a rickety *tabula plicata*, a tallow candle and a basin of clear water. The abbey certainly was not wealthy but everything was clean and the cell was well aired.

The chevalier put down his saddle-bags, sat down on the

mattress and took out a wax tablet and stylus. In the past he had shed light on a good many dark secrets, mysteries and cruel murders in his carvings on this soft white surface.

He stared thoughtfully at the rectangle of wax for some time as if it contained some inscription that only he could read, then he burrowed the stylus into the wax and traced the words 'Terre Gémétique'. What a strange name, thought the chevalier, did it come from the Latin *gemitus* or *gemere*, meaning a place of pain and groaning, or was it from *gemma*, the precious stone?

Then he drew a labyrinth and placed within it the names Odon, Arnulphe, Rurik, Joce and the monks of Jumièges . . .

'So,' he said, bent over the tablet, 'Odon is a "visitor". One of those *missi dominici* sent by high royal or ecclesiastical authority. Those "inquisitors" who interview the monks one by one, inspect the premises and follow the services in order to produce a report. If my memory serves me well, they are usually disliked by those who receive them, and some have even been stoned to death . . .'

And yet this sort of mission was not common, and Galeran thought that there must have been some sort of complaint or denunciation of very serious note for the Bishop to delegate Odon to the Terre Gémétique. He remembered the Prior's astonishment when Odon had introduced himself, and the enigmatic words that Odon had spoken to him: *Only he who wrote knows that I am coming.* Galeran understood by this that if there had been any sort of complaint, it must have come from the Prior himself. It certainly was not rare for rivalries to develop between abbots and priors, but it was a big step to call in an inquisitor!

A prior was an abbot's right hand and, as such, a very powerful figure within a monastery. It was well-known that such men were often consumed with the desire to overthrow their superiors. It was not insignificant that Saint Benoît himself was extremely reticent in his writings when it came to the need for such a role in his communities. In his wisdom, he preferred to have a council of elders, the *dizeniers*, and he was probably right, thought Galeran. But then all communities now had priors, and they were not all very godly men, far from it!

But what grounds for complaint had Jumièges's prior found

that justified the Bishop of Lisieux's obvious anxiety and his warnings?

And then there was Joce with his poor discoloured face and his bulging eyes. Joce *le Peor*, who was so terrified of the world that he had retreated from it only to meet a terrible death. Hard to tell whether Joce had been drowned and yet . . . The chevalier thought back over his injuries, it was as if he had scratched his neck before dying, except that his nails were bitten right down . . .

Galeran was now drawing a complex diagram, like a cathedral labyrinth, then abruptly he erased everything.

'Too soon!' he exclaimed, getting to his feet.

When he came out of his cell a little later, the bells were ringing for the Sext Mass.

8

The chevalier opened the little oak door and set off down a corridor that led to the dorter of the hostelry. He came across a monk ringing the death knell, calling the monks together around poor Brother Joce.

A little way away a dozen or so men, with breastplates showing beneath their light-coloured tunics, were discussing something animatedly. A young noble strutted amongst them, distinguishable by the richness of his attire and his haughty manner.

Father Baudri was going to have trouble ensuring that the rule of silence was observed by pilgrims who did not even respect the death knell, thought the chevalier. Here, no doubt, was the owner of the splendid palfrey, Rainolf de Clères, accompanied by his valets at arms.

In a corner, Galeran noticed a cot that was isolated from the others by heavy tenting, probably a traveller who was ill or dying, unless it was one of those who had been saved from the fatal fishing expedition. Fresh foliage was scattered across the floor of beaten earth, and a small brazier was trying in vain to heat the large room.

The chevalier went out into the paved courtyard and, revelling in the chill air, made his way over to the church dedicated to Notre-Dame. The Sext service had begun and the monks' voices could be heard vigorously intoning the *Veni creator*.

'Are you looking for someone, my Lord?' asked an old servant, dressed in a long surcoat of brown linen.

'Yes, my friend,' said the chevalier. 'I would like to see the Precentor, but I'm in no hurry. I will probably see him at the end of the service.'

'Are you the chevalier that arrived with the two monks earlier?'

'Quite so, but why this question, my friend?'

The old man rocked from one leg to the other. His face was so shrivelled that he looked like an apple that had spent a winter on the tree. His lips sketched a meagre smile: 'Oh! Forgive me, my Lord, and do not take my question in bad part. I was not thinking ill, but you could say it is my job to know who is who. I am the porter at Jumièges, you know. And, with all these comings and goings, and the deaths, and poor Joce . . .'

'There's no harm done,' said the chevalier smiling, 'but do you not wear the cloth?'

'Oh no, my Lord. I am a free man, my name is Tancard. My father and my father's father, and his father before him were porters here. I am well on in years and my son will take over from me soon, if he so wishes.'

The chevalier nodded, and the old man continued morosely, 'It is a fine duty that we do, and one that our fathers were proud to undertake . . .'

'Does your son have no wish to undertake it?'

'Oh, I wouldn't know about that, my Lord, he's still young. Whereas I have been on this earth nearly 75 years! He was from my second marriage-bed, my wife was still young and fresh and she bore fruit . . . She died of it, poor lamb. He's only eighteen and all he can talk about is horses, he must have come and taken your horses.'

'His name is Roderic, is that right? Fie, fie, he seemed a good young man, and yes, it is true that he knows about horses. Did you know Brother Joce well?'

'Ah, yes, he was kind but more timid than a virgin, may God forgive me. He never wanted to set foot outside the walls, except for processions.'

'And the Prior?'

The Porter's face darkened, 'The Abbot Eustache is a godly man but the Prior, I'd rather not say too much on the subject . . . By my faith, he runs Jumièges as if the Abbot were no longer here. I do not know many who agree with him, except perhaps for Gachelin.'

'The Sexton?'

'Yes, they're often together those two, like crows on a branch. But, forgive me, I do not know how to hold my tongue. Don't tell anyone that I have told you all this.'

'Nay, nay, Tancard, I will be mute as a rock. I will stay at the Porter's lodge until the mass is finished and, as I still do not know anyone, it would be useful if you would name those we see, whether they be monks or visitors.'

'That I most certainly will, my Lord. Come and sit down, I have a little wooden bench in the sun, here, up against the wall of my lodge. We'll be more comfortable there,' said the old man, delighted to have found someone with whom he could talk.

9

Two young girls were sitting on the edge of the abbey's vivarium where the monks kept hundreds of prettily speckled fish. They liked this peaceful corner where they were sheltered from unwanted observers by a beech hedge.

For the moment, the two girls were completely wrapped up in their conversation and had little thought for the trout that darted like streaks of silver in the limpid water of the pond.

'You can't do a thing like that. Don't you see? You are betrothed, and anyway everyone here hates him.'

The brunette who was talking was flushed with rage and her eyes shone angrily.

'Oh, Mabille, calm down. He loves me, do you hear. He wants to marry me,' retorted her friend.

'To marry you! You are betrothed to another, as far as I know. No one here would be prepared to conduct such a marriage. And what is your Aunt Arda going to have to say about it? Stop playing, I beg you, Edel. You do tease these men too much, and that's not kind.'

Edel looked up at her friend, who noticed that her grey-green eyes were brimming with tears. Her heavy golden tresses came right down to her hips, and her features were so fine that she looked like the holy Virgin on an altarpiece. She pinched her lips, bit back her tears and stood up angrily.

'There, you see, you're just like the others, you do not love me enough to help me!' she said in a strident voice.

'That's not true, Edel, you're being unfair. But I do not want to help you throw yourself into the arms of a man who is not right for you, a brutal man, and a foreigner to cap it all.'

'What do you know about him, anyway?' rejoined Edel.

'What I know is that we're not children any more and that it is time to stop your foolish games,' said Mabille getting to her feet.

'I agree with you and that's why I want to marry a man, a real one, not some boy like Roderic or a withered old has-been.'

'But why not choose someone who would really suit you?' sighed Mabille. 'Hey, did you see the chevalier who came across on the ferry earlier?'

'Of course I saw him,' said Edel sulkily.

'Well, is not he handsome, then? Doesn't he look like a real man as you say?'

Edel shrugged her slender shoulders: 'Well, he's not bad, but I have seen better . . .'

Then she wheedled, 'Mabille, dear heart, be good to me, help me just once more, please, it'll be the last time.'

Mabille sighed. The two of them had been raised together and Edel got what she wanted every time. Mabille eventually gave in to her friend's smiles and cajoling. When all was said and done, the little minx treated her as she did the boys, thought Mabille, already resigned. It was, anyway, always Edel that the boys preferred, that they found pretty and to whom they paid court. Edel, the beautiful Edel with her long golden braids.

'I'm going to think about it,' said Mabille who did not want to be seen to give in straight away.

'Oh, you are an angel. Oh, my sweet, how I love you, I love you more than anyone in the world,' cried Edel, clapping her hands together.

'I haven't said yes yet,' grumbled the brunette.

Edel took her in her arms and smothered her cheeks with kisses.

'Oh yes you did say yes, oh yes you did.'

Mabille sighed and, tearing herself away from her friend's cajoling, she walked a few paces away.

'What is it that you want me to do, Edel?'

'Right, you know who I'm afraid of, do you not?' she whispered.

'Yes. Look, that's another one, if you hadn't behaved as you did, if you hadn't led him on, if you hadn't accepted his gifts . . . !'

'Stop your sermons, will you! All I ask is for you to keep an eye on him.'

'Oh, is that all?'

'Please!' begged Edel.

'And once you're married, what are you going to do about old Aunt Arda?'

'I won't do anything different, my sweet. Anyway, the old dear is half deaf. She spends all her time with her nose in her needlework, and when she's not stitching she's sleeping! I'll be able to go off and join my husband quite happily at nightfall. And when we have enough money to leave, we'll go to Sicily.'

'To Sicily, but where on earth is Sicily?'

'In the Orient, I think. Well, I'm not really sure, but it is a long way away and it is beautiful, that's all I know.'

Mabille let out a long sigh:

'I do not like it. You do not seem to realise . . . For someone as fragile as you to travel such a long way . . . And what if your husband begets you a child straight away, what would you do then?'

'Oh, I'd go and see old Ingegerde. She knows what to do to stop women carrying their babes.' Then Edel burst into a pearly little laugh. 'Without her I would have had a babe in arms long hence!'

'What are you saying, you're mad?'

'Oh you really can be so naïve! I have known for a long time how to lie with a man without begetting a child.'

'Oh Edel! How could you do that, it is a great sin, a mortal sin! Are you not afraid of damnation?'

'I'll do my penitence when I'm old!'

'And what if you died suddenly?'

Edel burst out laughing again and said playfully, 'Don't worry so much, my sweet, I'm in very good health.'

'Be that as it may,' said Mabille gravely, 'does your future husband know that he is not the first?'

'Oh no! He would kill me if he realised,' said Edel, suddenly afraid.

'Now you see that I'm right, what are you going to do on your wedding night?'

'I'll behave like a virgin in his arms, I'll scream and cry and spill a little rabbit blood. He shall not know a thing, I can assure you, he is so much in love.'

'Edel, my poor Edel, all this is lies and wickedness, and I'm much afeared for you. I will help you, but this will be the last time. Never again, by Our Lady, I swear it.'

And the brunette strode off, leaving her pretty friend rooted to the spot in stunned silence.

10

After Compline, the final service at the end of the day, the bell had begun to toll for the special mass for the dead. The villagers and fishermen, headed by the mourners, had processed to the church of Notre-Dame for the funeral service. During his sermon, the Abbot Eustache had announced that thenceforward the abbey would provide for the wives and orphans of the villagers killed in the hunt. When the service was over, the bodies were interred in the parish cemetery and the crowd dispersed.

In accordance with custom, the unfortunate Joce had been wrapped in his cloth mat and buried by the Benedictine brothers in the monastic garden of Jumièges, there to find the rest that he had sought so desperately during his short life.

All the bells had stopped ringing and a heavy silence had descended on the great abbey. The sun shot its last rays out across the Seine. The wind was blowing in from the sea ever more strongly, spreading the foul stench of the whale's carcass, which still lay on the shore.

The ancient chronicles said that in the Terre Gémétique it had been the custom, ever since the abbey was founded, to have a celebratory feast after the great hunt.

When news spread that the beast had been put to death, men and women had come running from the surrounding hamlets to make the most of this good fortune, offering a helping hand to cut up the carcass in exchange for a square meal. That night every one, even the poorest, would eat their fill. The villagers, happy to be alive still, could think of nothing but their revelries, and tried to forget the poor souls that they had just committed to the earth.

A group of peasants stood discussing something heatedly in front of a cottage. A woman who had just lost her first born son in the hunt did not want to go with her friends. She was standing on the threshold of the house, her face blank, her eyes dry from too much crying, and with her arms crossed over her ragged clothes. Her husband was trying in vain to persuade her to come, when one of her neighbours, a fat woman with a child clamped to her breast, burst out, 'What do the dead matter, we should make the most of the good that comes to us, then what will be will be! Your children have still got to eat, Berthe, it is not every day that they can fill their bellies. If you do not want to go, we'll take them along, won't we?'

'Yup, my old love,' muttered the husband, 'she's right. Let's go and eat before we get eaten by the worms.' And leaving the poor woman alone with her sorrow, the whole gaggle of them set off towards the banquet, the father forcibly dragging the children who had wanted to stay with their mother.

Long tables had been set under a clump of beech trees. In the centre of the area three long ditches had been filled with burning embers on which enormous cooking pots bubbled. They gave off an appetising aroma of fish and herbs.

Not far away, peasant women sat before improvised stoves cooking large brown pancakes which they piled on to platters of woven strips of willow. Children ran over to the tables with them, gobbling up snippets on the way. The youngest, oblivious to the noise and activity around them, played with spinning tops and jacks in their midst.

As was customary on this sort of occasion, a dozen barrels of wine from Conihout had been donated by Abbot Eustache. They had barely been lifted down from the carts before the villagers had heaved them onto blocks of wood and tapped them.

In the monastery, the Abbot had authorised the servants to stop working after mass, and the good souls were stumbling over each other to get out of the walled enclosure. The chevalier, who was on his way back to his cell, found himself carried along by the bustle.

'And a very good evening to you, my Lord. Will you come revelling with us in the village?'

Galeran turned round and recognised the young groom from the abbey.

'A good evening to you, Roderic. Why not? Perhaps you could act as my guide for the occasion.'

'Gladly, my Lord. Come, the meal is held on the big square. When the weather's right, we set up the tables on the beach, but it is too hot for that and, despite the wind, there's a terrible stench next to the beast. You can smell it right up here. Luckily it'll all be burned up soon.'

Lord Rainolf of Clères and his men at arms had also deserted the hostelry and you could safely wager that there would not be many in the frater that evening.

Men were coming out of their houses, slamming the doors behind them, their children at their heels. The girls had put on clean head-wraps, and had woven ribbons in their hair, and the boys were in tunics of blue cloth. After the banquet they would be dancing and carousing with the maidens.

Giving way to a group of youngsters who were running breathlessly past them, the chevalier and his young companion took the white path that led to the hamlet. The blacksmith was still toiling in his workshop and, as they came closer, they heard the rhythmic ringing of the hammer on the anvil. The forge was huge, and the two men stopped to look at the fused metal bending under the succession of accurate blows. His face reddened by the fire and his brow gleaming with sweat, the smith was working on a heavy chain. His helper, a boy of about ten whose face was as scarlet as his own, was working the bellows proudly.

'Good day to you,' said Roderic with a tilt of his head.

'Hello, son. Your knife is ready,' said the smith without even taking his eyes off his work.

'Many thanks, Landric. I'll take it tomorrow, or perhaps this evening. Are you coming to the feast?'

'Later, I still have work to do for the abbey, it is urgent as far as I have been told, and night is falling fast.'

Galeran and his companion set off again. Darkness was falling and they could see torches being lit in the distance.

11

Long before they reached the square, the two men could already hear shouting and laughter. The revelries had hardly begun and already the ruddy-faced villagers were competing to empty the flasks of wine distributed by the boys.

A hefty labourer from Heurteauville stood with his belt undone, urinating as he drank, causing great hilarity amongst the villagers. Two serious-looking boys sat cross-legged putting down a pebble for each flask that was emptied, betting that the man would not be able to hold another. On the thirtieth pebble, the man lifted his head, burped loudly, cast a haggard eye round his audience, and collapsed in the dust with his arms spread out. His heavy cheeks were soon quivering with the vibrations of his noisy snoring.

The crowds burst out laughing and then dispersed. The boys, disappointed, moved off to look for another wager somewhere else.

'The living quickly forget the dead, do they not, my Lord?' whispered the young Roderic.

'Yes,' said the chevalier thoughtfully. 'In their unhappiness, they prefer inebriation to visions of heaven, and one can hardly blame them.'

Along the tables, the women from the village were serving up soup to the poor and the elderly. People gave way respectfully before the chevalier, greeting Roderic as he passed.

The fishermen, with their hands covered in blood, were cutting great hunks of flesh that the women came to fetch for cooking.

'It is strange,' observed the chevalier, 'it is like beef, not like fish at all.'

'Have you never eaten it?'

'By my faith, no. I did not even think it was edible. It is true that the whales I have seen in Léonnais were beached.

Those that were still whole were hardly appetising. Their fat and their baleen was used, and the rest was given to the dogs.'

'Come, let's sit here,' said Roderic, pushing through the crowd with his elbows.

The two men sat down on the end of a long log bench. A young girl put before them some pancakes and two bowls of soup with whale meat floating in them.

'You'll see, it is not at all bad but it loses a lot of water in the cooking, that's why the women boil it in stock. They know how to cook it. You mustn't roast it, otherwise it becomes so tough you can't get a knife into it.'

Just as they were finishing their bowls, a beautiful blonde girl came over towards them and greeted Roderic with a wink of her eye. She had fine, delicate features and astonishing grey-green eyes. She tapped the ground impatiently with her pretty little foot in its dainty shoe.

'Well then, have you lost your tongue, Roderic?' said the girl. 'You could introduce me to my Lord chevalier, I would have thought.'

The young man gulped in surprise and turned to Galeran, stammering: 'Um yes. My Lord, allow me to introduce Damsel Edel.'

The chevalier, amused by his young companion's confusion, greeted the pretty girl.

'They call me Galeran de Lesneven, gentle damsel.'

'Where are you from, my Lord chevalier?' said Edel who was unashamedly examining the young man from head to foot.

'From the ends of the earth, from Léon country, my lovely,' replied the chevalier addressing his blue-eyed stare at Edel.

The young girl blushed, but did not lower her head and went on with great aplomb: 'Tell me, Chevalier, you must know where the Orient is?'

'What a strange question, would you be planning to go there, gentle Edel?'

'And why not?' said the young girl defiantly.

'The journey is long and perilous, fair damsel, and requires experienced companions. You have to reach the furthest parts of Italy and from there take a ship which risks frequent attacks from pirates and Moors.'

The young girl opened her beautiful eyes wide.

During the conversation Roderic was watching her glumly. Unable to bear it any longer, he cried out. 'What do you mean, talking about the Orient? You're going mad. Edel, my poor Edel, what have you gone and dreamed up now?'

'I'm not *your* Edel, Roderic the groom. I am Damsel Edel and I won't have trouble finding a companion to take me as far as the Orient!'

With these words, uttered in a shrill voice, the damsel left the two young men and made off with pert self-assurance, arrogantly swinging her pretty rump.

Roderic breathed a heartbreaking sigh and turned to the chevalier:

'Forgive her, my Lord, she's as sharp as a needle, my Edel, she's still young but she's not malicious at heart. A child is a child.'

Nor gentle nor generous either, my poor friend, thought the chevalier to himself. That sort of beauty devours your heart and body far more than it satisfies them.

A monk leaning on one of the tables a little distance away had followed the exchange and had watched every move of Edel's graceful form. He was a sturdy fellow with a square jaw, more cut out for a suit of armour than a habit.

Sensing that he was being watched, Galeran looked up and met his eye. The monk stared at him for a moment, then turned on his heel and disappeared amongst the villagers.

'Who is that strapping monk?' asked the chevalier.

'Oh, he's Brother Gachelin.'

The young man had paled again and could not take his eyes off the spot where the monk had been swallowed up by the crowd.

'Sexton of Jumièges?'

'Yes, my Lord, the very same.'

'You hardly seem to hold him dear, tell me?'

'No, that I do not,' retorted Roderic heatedly. Then, lowering his voice, he added, 'He is not worthy of his monk's robes.'

'What do you mean?'

'He has the funeral rights of this parish and of Le Mesnil, and he's succeeded in gathering so much money that he's gone and bought himself a house with servants outside the monastery. I'm not even sure whether the Abbot knows about it.'

'What are these funeral rights?'

'Oh, it is as old as the abbey. Every time someone dies, the Sexton has the right to take the deceased's best garment and one third of his furniture, that's all! And him, he often takes more. He apparently even stole the last belongings of some poor old woman who was too afraid to complain.'

'And he has a house of his own?'

'Indeed. Up on the heights on the way to the pest-house, a proper house built of stone. And there's something else about that monk, he's got an eye for the girls, and they say that he's sent more than one to her confinement.'

'That's a serious accusation, Roderic. Are you thinking of Edel, and are you not just a little too jealous?'

'Why, no my Lord, I just see what's there to be seen, that's all.'

12

The feast had been going on for several hours. The children and youngsters were tired of sitting and their legs were itching to move. They started to chant: 'We're going to dance! We're going to dance!'

In a meadow not far from the square, a large platform of wood was put up onto four barrels and two travelling musicians were lifted up onto this improvised stage.

One of them started playing a two-time tune on his rebec, and the other accompanied him with a reedy sound from his flute.

Straight away the youngsters took their places, concentrating hard. They formed two alternate rows of men and women, holding hands as they faced each other, tapping out the rhythm on the ground with their feet.

Then, the two lines of men turned to each other and mixed together, each man exchanging his partner and coming back to his place with his new partner.

Edel was radiant, going gracefully from one hand to the other, as if she did not want to miss a single minute of such pleasure. She was the prettiest girl there, and she took on life with great gusto. But there was also something sinister in the air, as if some evil hovered about her. Edel knew that everyone was looking at her, but she did not know that not everyone looked at her admiringly or even kindly . . . the men that she had taken pleasure in duping, the jealous women who had been abandoned for her, and the elderly who sat a little further away under the beeches, peevishly watching their offspring carousing.

'Have you seen that little Edel, who does she think she is?'

'A cat on heat . . .' goaded one of the old men, digging his neighbour in the ribs and letting out a little laugh.

'Her father was not up to much,' said one toothless old woman, 'and as for her mother . . .'

*

The Dane had just arrived at the revelries and he too devoured the pretty blonde with his eyes.

Galeran thought to himself that poor Roderic was going to have his hands full with his little beauty and all her suitors. Rurik the Dane would certainly make a richer and more seductive suitor than the little groom from Jumièges. Furthermore, Rurik was an unusually good-looking man. With his blond hair gleaming in the firelight and his handsome jaw clamped tensely shut, he did not take his eyes off Edel's leaping form. His oiled muscles rippled under his leather tunic, inspiring respect in the villagers who stared at him resentfully, not daring to speak to him. Nevertheless, tension was mounting around the foreigner. The men were gathering into little groups and some of the women were spitting on the ground.

The Dane shrugged his shoulders, threw one last glance at Edel, who had just stopped dancing with a breathless giggle, and moved away.

'Would you be my partner for this dance, my Lord? They're just about to start dancing the chain?'

Galeran looked up. A dark-haired girl was standing in front of him smiling shyly. She was wearing a modest auburn kirtle that was a little worn on the sleeves, and her feet were bare.

'Why not?' said the chevalier. 'But first of all tell me your name, gentle maiden, and tell me why you do me the honour of asking me.'

'Oh, do not make fun of me, my Lord,' she said gently, making as if to leave.

The chevalier held out his hand to stop her.

'I assure you I am not, fair damsel!'

She smiled again and gave a little curtsey.

'I am called Mabille, my Lord, and if I came it was because you were alone.'

'It is true,' thought the chevalier, oddly moved, 'alone and, above all, anxious amidst this rabble of dancers and Roderic has gone off to nurse his sorrows elsewhere.'

In the distance, men were brandishing torches. The musicians jumped down from the stage and the men hurried to their partners. The chevalier leapt nimbly to his feet and led Mabille to join in. They all set off, following the musicians, hand in hand, turning, pushing, singing and running across the meadows and the flatlands. The elderly, still sitting under their trees, watched the torches of the joyous procession disappearing into the night, and drank and chatted as they waited for it to return.

After some time, they saw a hazy light in the distance and heard something that sounded like a cavalry charge gradually coming closer until the musicians appeared again followed by the whole tumbling crowd of dancers who came helter-skelter into the meadow and collapsed on the grass.

The chevalier helped his little partner back to her feet. Out of breath and glowing with perspiration, they were both laughing without really knowing why.

In the distance the abbey bells rang for Nocturn.

'It is getting late, gentle Mabille,' said the chevalier as he came back to himself, 'and I must leave you. I have very much enjoyed dancing with you.'

'Are you staying in Father Baudri's hostelry?' asked Mabille, flushing.

'Yes, inquisitive damsel,' said the chevalier, planting a gentle kiss on her dimpled little hand. 'But is there anyone who can take you back to your door quite safely?'

'Indeed yes, my Lord, my young brother is waiting for me under the beeches over there. He doesn't really like dancing.'

'He will soon, never fear. So, all's well then. May God keep you, Mabille,' said the chevalier, turning away.

'Chevalier!'

'Yes.'

'We have danced together and I do not even know your name,' she whispered, lowering her eyes.

'It is true. My name is Galeran de Lesneven, gentle Mabille. May God protect you.'

'And may Our Lady watch over you, my Lord Galeran.'

The young girl curtseyed briefly and hurried off silently with her younger brother at her heels.

It was dark. As she ran home, Mabille was smiling to herself. She, who was so shy and so poor, whom no one ever asked to dance, whom no one even looked at and who always lived in Edel's shadow, how had she dared to speak to the handsome chevalier? Mabille shook her head. She knew the answer: if he had not looked so lonely and so sad she would never have dared . . .

'There you are, you poor thing, you're never going to change,' she sighed as she reached her humble house and climbed through the narrow window to the communal room, which had been left open.

Inside, everyone was asleep and, like her younger brother, she felt her way tentatively to her mattress.

Apart from a few forgotten drunkards snoring peacefully under the tables, everyone had gone and the square was deserted. Only the dogs slunk around looking for scraps.

An extinguished torch had been planted into the earth. The chevalier picked it up and lit it from the embers in one of the ditches, before deciding to go back up to the abbey.

Half-way there, when he could just see the outline of the first houses, he shivered and stopped, perfectly alert, with his hand on his dagger. A dark shape was moving under cover of the trees. The chevalier raised his torch and frowned. It looked like the outline of a man on all fours. The trees were creaking in the wind and the stillness of the night was interrupted by a long wail.

Galeran started walking again, listening out for the least sound. But the wail, more animal than human, was not repeated; the silhouette dived into the darkness and disappeared. The chevalier soon reached the shadows of the abbey walls and, when he had knocked several times on the oak door, the Porter's sleepy face appeared at the hatch.

'Oh, it is you, Chevalier, come in, come in.'

Galeran wished the old man a good night before returning to the hostelry. He crossed the dorter and noticed that, with the exception of the bed in the corner, the entire room was empty. Not one of the travellers had yet come to bed that beautiful September night.

13

When he struck her the second time, she tripped and fell against the wooden wall. Her cheek was marked with the burning imprint of his hand, and she was crying hot tears, raising her arm to protect herself.

Her linen shift was torn to reveal her graceful body. The Dane was half naked, pacing up and down the room like a wild animal. He looked so handsome like this, consumed with anger. Edel suddenly realised just how much she did love him and just how truly she had lost him.

'Accursed woman, you had no right to do this to me! I want you to tell me who it is, so that I can slit his throat before your very eyes. Do you hear me!'

She trembled. Rurik's mouth was twisted into a fierce snarl. Edel felt deadly fear insinuating itself into her belly. And to think that she had thought she would be able to dupe him. She had never seen such a look of hatred on his face.

Horrified, she gulped and spoke with difficulty:

'I beg you, Rurik, he raped me, I swear by Our Lady, and I was so in love with you . . .'

'By my troth, you are lying!' roared Rurik. 'You are no despoiled maiden. You're lying in the name of the Virgin. You were playing the little virgin in my arms, you were making fun of me, little whore . . . making fun of me!'

'No, no, I was so afraid that you would reject me. No, believe me, for pity's sake . . .'

'I would have done better to have overpowered you in a ditch like some dumb beast, do you understand!' he said seizing her by her hair. 'Who is it? do you hear, are you going to tell me?'

He shook her by her long plaits, forcing her to get back to her feet. She felt weak, suddenly so weak that she did not even try to defend herself and stood with the tears streaming down her cheeks.

'I'll tell you!' she sobbed. 'Stop, for pity's sake, you're hurting me.'

He looked at her and then let go abruptly. She fell at his feet, pitiably.

'Is it that little good-for-nothing Roderic? Did you give yourself to him?' roared the Dane.

Edel hesitated. She heard something snap outside and turned whiter than death.

The Dane had heard it too. He put on his leather hunting cape, grabbed his axe, went silently over to the door and opened it. Someone or something ran off into the forests.

Rurik threw one last glance at Edel and set off in pursuit of the creature.

The miserable girl threw herself at the door and closed it as she wept.

She was terrified and she fell with her back against the door but, as she did, she had time to see the shutter across the room from her slowly opening before she lost consciousness.

PART TWO

'For ever and ever in this life,
So long as the golden moon shines,
I will not take of this drink
Before I see my loved one;
Is my beloved ready,
she for whom I have waited so long?'

The Kalevala, *verse XIX*
Finnish epic

14

The torches burned, throwing their nimble shadows over the whitewashed walls. It was not yet daylight when the old priest from the parish of Jumièges came before the Abbot Eustache. He had asked for an audience, and this in itself was so unusual that the Abbot had received him immediately in the chapter house before going to Nocturn.

The Abbot was pacing up and down the room, his face lined with weariness, and the old priest thought that this agitation in Father Eustache was provoked by his visit. He was mistaken. The Abbot had plenty of concerns this morning in addition to this minor disruption to his routine. He listened only distractedly to the old churchman's words, and his inattention was to have a sorry effect on subsequent events.

'Reverend Father Abbot, I asked to see you before Nocturn because something very worrying happened to me during the night, and I wanted to confide in you and let you, in your great wisdom, handle the matter.'

The old man wrung his hands in his anxiety and his voice trembled slightly. The Abbot came to an abrupt halt directly in front of the old priest: 'Speak, my brother, I am listening,' he said gravely.

'I went to bed late because of the feasting and rejoicing. I went to sleep straight after hearing the bells ringing Nocturn. I was woken suddenly by the sound of someone knocking on the church door. I got up and half opened the door. Then I heard a man's voice speaking this sacred passage clearly and loudly: "With this ring I thee wed, with my body I thee honour."

'The woman hung back behind the man, who was tall and well-built, and her face was hidden by a crimson veil. She held out her hand and he put the ring onto her finger before I could stop him or shut the door.'

'You did not recognise them? Who on earth could have wanted to get married in secret?'

'I know not, Father Abbot, it was not yet day and the man wore his capuchon lowered over his face.'

'What did you do, then?'

'I blessed them, Reverend Father. May God forgive me if I did wrong, I cannot rest for thinking of it.'

The Abbot turned away, looked out of the window and let out a deep sigh, almost as if he were relieved. 'Right or wrong, my brother, as you well know, by pronouncing that passage before you they were married before God our Saviour and you could do nothing to alter that.'

'Yes, but . . .' the old man protested feebly.

'Go in peace, my brother, and trust in God's infinite wisdom rather than what wisdom I may have,' interrupted the Abbot.

'But, Reverend, there may have been some kind of deception involved . . .'

'I do not wish to believe it, my brother. It was probably just two children who love each other and whose parents would not consent to their marriage.'

'May our Saviour hear your wishes, Reverend Father,' said the old priest, bowing to the Abbot before withdrawing reluctantly.

Abbot Eustache waited until he had left before allowing himself to collapse into a chair. He ran his hand over his forehead; he felt so very tired. The responsibility for so many souls weighed on him a little more heavily every day.

He kept going over in his mind the moment when the monks had elected him 'with one voice'. He had protested in front of the whole assembly: *non sum dignus*, I am not worthy.

But the monks had not listened to his protestations, and had carried him all the way to the Abbot's chair. He had now borne this thorn in his side for four years. Four long years in which he had tried to be worthy of such a duty, and in which he found only too often that he was surrounded by evil, lies, hatred or vanity.

He loathed power. He was not suited to high authority and abhorred its consequences. Those close to him had changed their attitude towards him overnight. Some had become servile, trying to win his favour, others had become distant, reserved, poorly disguising their resentment, their disappointed ambitions, their hopes of compromising his position or even – who knows? – of catching him out.

And now, this visitor Odon, had been sent by the Bishop of Lisieux. What sort of calumny had been brought to bear for Arnulphe to despatch his monk to Jumièges? On top of everything else, there was the matter of his seal . . .

That night, while the festive fires still blazed in the village, the Abbot had written a long letter to the Bishop, asking for an explanation for the visitor's arrival. He wanted to know the reason for it, and why Arnulphe had not seen fit to warn him of the visit.

Taking the white wax, he had unlocked his metal strongbox to take out the *sigillum*, the official mark of his power. But the box was empty. There was nothing on the red velvet cushion, his personal seal had disappeared. Until it was found again, he could sign no official documents, not even this letter to the Bishop of Lisieux.

Furthermore, he would be forced to announce this incredible disappearance during the chapter that very morning, in front of the assembled monks and – inevitably – in front of the visiting monk.

The Abbot had still not made up his mind how to go about this when a young novice came to fetch him for Nocturn.

15

Mabille woke with a jump and suddenly remembered the promise she had made to Edel the day before.

She crept discreetly from her humble home, almost before dawn had broken, and slipped away to the isolated house where Edel lived with her elderly aunt.

As she neared her friend's house she saw straight away that something was wrong. There was a small gathering of people and, in their midst, she recognised Arda, Edel's old aunt, who was talking loudly and agitatedly. She wanted Drogtegand, the village elder, to be alerted because her niece had disappeared, she had not been home all night.

Instinctively, Mabille hid behind a thicket of holly to listen. She must warn Edel before the villagers found her in her lover's arms. They were all going to set out to search for her, led by Roderic, her betrothed, and Mabille dared not think what they might do if they found the two of them together.

After a moment's hesitation, she decided to go over to Rurik's house, and she started running towards the upper part of the village, slipping behind the cottages and using the tracks that backed on to the vegetable plots.

Why did Edel choose that wretched Dane? He's so different from all of us. The people hate him, they still remember the devastation caused by the 'scourges of the Lord' with their long-ships. And the worst of it was that Rurik, like his ancestors, had a taste for warfare and was always thumbing his nose at the locals. And now he'd gone and taken the prettiest girl in the village, the one all the young men wanted! thought Mabille as she hurried along.

Once she was beyond the abbey, she cut across the woods towards the pest-house. The day was going to be gloomy, the equinoctial winds were stirring the boughs of the trees, rustling their leaves.

Like most of the villagers, Mabille was not keen to venture here for fear of coming across a leper, or even just hearing the mournful bell that announced their dreaded arrival.

She stopped for a moment, out of breath, but she was stubborn . . . her father certainly grumbled about her stubbornness often enough. She had decided that she would find her friend and she remembered that the Abbot had lent the Dane a little house not far from the pest-house. Edel had described it to her and she thought that she would probably recognise it.

She jumped suddenly: a dark silhouette had appeared where the track turned a corner. She screwed up her eyes and then relaxed, it was a Benedictine monk making his way back towards the abbey. When he drew level with her, Mabille shyly sketched the sign of the cross, but the monk did not bless her and walked by without noticing her, his face buried in his cloak, probably lost in thought.

There was still no house. Mabille was beginning to regret venturing so far from home, when she saw a path leading to a clearing thick with weeds, and in the middle of the clearing an ill-kept cottage. A fence of woven gorse protected an abandoned vegetable plot. The place was steeped in silence.

With her heart in her mouth, Mabille stepped slowly closer, hesitating to go any further. She made the sign of the cross again and called timidly: 'Edel, Edel, it is me.'

Soon she had reached the door, but she dared not knock.

'Rurik, Edel, it is me, Mabille,' she said in a voice that shook with fear.

Apart from the wind that kept slamming a shutter somewhere to the back of the building, nothing seemed to be moving inside.

Then Mabille noticed that the door was ajar. After a moment's hesitation, she gently pushed at it with the tips of her bare toes, and it opened with a creak.

The interior seemed terrifyingly dark and Mabille's shadow stretched out in the rectangle of light from the doorway. Once her eyes were used to the darkness, she moved forward, gingerly. She was greeted by the stench of wet leather, of fat and smoke. She was in the Dane's tannery. The wilted leaves that covered the floor of beaten earth had drifted into piles that smelled of autumnal decay.

Sections of baleen and strips of skin, with which Rurik made bows, had been put to dry by the chimney where a few embers were still glowing. In one corner of the large room was a pile of fox and wolf pelts. Not far from there, the bows and quivers were neatly stacked, along with the lances that he used for the whale hunts. Each weapon was carefully cleaned and oiled. Along the walls, axes glinted menacingly. Mabille had trouble imagining Edel, so refined and coquettish, in this hunter's lair.

Seeing no sign of her friend, she was about to leave when she noticed the bed. Curtained off by a faded drape, the Dane's bed was in the furthest corner of the room. Mabille went over slowly and drew back the curtain. Counterpanes of various furs lay in heaps on the floor next to an old mattress that spewed out its straw stuffing. The only shutter in the room was swinging violently back and forth, letting light into the room intermittently.

Whether it was the sound of the shutter, the way the counterpanes lay in shreds or the smell of decay, the young girl froze, overwhelmed by a nameless fear. She turned on her heels and ran out, leaving the door wide open behind her.

When she felt that she was far enough away from the Dane's house she slowed down a little and then stopped. A little further ahead she saw the dark outline of the sanatorium at the pesthouse.

Trying to catch her breath and to reason with herself, she noticed a little hillock surrounded by trees and she decided to rest there for a few minutes. When she had pushed her way through the branches, she slipped between the bushes and dropped down onto a mossy rock.

With her head in her hands she set about gathering her thoughts. 'What can have happened to stop Edel going home? Where on earth can she be now? Had she already set off for the Orient with Rurik?'

She shrugged her slender shoulders, 'No! that could not be right! Edel had told her . . . she did not want to leave straight away. But then that bed, that ripped mattress, as if there had been a fight, and the house left open to the four winds.'

Suddenly, a terrible thought struck her. She remembered what her friend had confided in her, how she had been so sure of herself, sure that she could deceive the whole world . . . Perhaps Rurik had turned out to be not quite as naïve as the others and he had found out what his beloved was capable of.

Mabille shivered. The rising sun was already peeping through the leaves, and the young girl, gradually noticing her surroundings, realised that it must be getting late and that her family would begin worrying.

Not knowing how she could now warn Edel, she decided it was time to go back to the hamlet and, without saying anything, to join in the search with the other villagers.

The wind was blowing more and more powerfully, snatching leaves from the high branches. The young girl stood up and wiped her hands on her smock.

Suddenly she noticed some crows overhead, circling ever closer in the grey sky.

Two of them landed at once behind a thicket.

Mabille had come to a halt, wondering what could be attracting these scavengers.

'Probably a dead animal,' she said to herself nervously. 'I hate those birds, they bring bad luck!'

More crows came and perched on nearby trees, cawing angrily.

She was about to run off when she noticed something red quivering in the bushes, buffeted by the gusts of wind.

She moved closer and saw that it was a long trail of scarlet hooked onto the thorns. She tried in vain to pull at it. It looked as if it came from another piece of material behind the bushes. Giving in to her curiosity, Mabille decided to find it, and she made her way through the thicket.

Furious at being disturbed, the crows flew off on heavy wings and there, suddenly, in the half light Mabille saw the body of a young woman lying amongst the bushes. She was small and her face was covered by a red veil.

Wide-eyed with horror, Mabille moved closer and stared at each mutilated limb, the fragile skin under the shredded, bloodied remnants of her shift . . . but the most terrifying thing was the gaping wound between her breasts. Her whole trunk had been carved open as if with one stroke of an axe, and the ten-inch wound went all the way down to her stomach, laying bare some of her ribs.

Mabille bit her lips so hard that she drew blood, but she did not even notice. She moved her trembling hand towards the veil that masked the neck and face of the body. Heavy golden locks strayed from beneath it and, without wanting to believe it, Mabille already knew who she was going to find.

She pulled and the red veil, the veil with which a bride covers her head, fell from her hand. It looked as if a wolf had laid into Edel's white throat, tearing it with its great teeth. The blood had dried, daubing the chin with splashes of black that were now swarming with ants. The beautiful, bewitching Edel stared up at Mabille, her grey-green eyes filled with terror and her mouth deformed by a snarl of appalling pain.

Quaking in every limb, Mabille heard someone screaming and eventually understood that it was she herself, but she could not stop, nor could she tear her eyes away from the tortured body of her friend whose wounds were teaming with insects.

Still screaming, she fled, running like a mad woman, oblivious to the branches scratching her face. When she reached the hatch of the pest-house, she drummed her hands on the door screaming all the louder, battering her small hands on the heavy iron studs before she slipped to the ground in a faint.

When she came to, Mabille was lying on a bed of straw. The Friar Nurse was watching her anxiously. A monk stood behind him, waiting for orders.

The young girl was shaking in every limb, she looked at the two men without seeing them and when she opened her mouth it was to scream all over again. She tried to speak but, finding that she could not, she screamed all the louder. Hideous images of Edel's body danced around her, just as the crows had circled round the body earlier. She flailed her arms around to drive them away, throwing off the men who were trying to hold her up. With the help of the monk, the nurse, who was holding her head, managed to slip a potion made of poppy sap between her clenched teeth. Mabille lost consciousness again.

16

The long corridor led to a narrow, studded oak door. The novice indicated that Galeran should go in and slipped away without a sound.

Once he had lifted the latch, the door opened silently to reveal the long expanse of the library where Father Foulques, the Precentor of Jumièges, who was responsible for the scriptorium, was waiting for him.

The narrow windows overlooking the cloisters threw a meagre light over the desks at which monks were studying.

There were tablets fixed to the walls to house rows of bound volumes and rolled manuscripts. Some rarer works were chained, so that they could not be stolen. Galeran learned later that one of the librarian monks, the *thesaurarius* or guardian of the treasure, held the keys.

The whole place was bathed in an atmosphere of peace, troubled only by the lazy buzzing of flies. Here, more than anywhere else, the rule of silence was rigorously observed and no dialogue was acceptable except by signs and in writing.

'*Taciturnitas virtutes plurimas nutrit*, silence nurtures all virtues,' thought the chevalier with a smile, as he moved quietly to the middle of the room.

Father Foulques was monitoring the progress of two young novices who were studiously deciphering Guillaume de Saint-Thierry's *De Contemplado Deo*.

The chevalier looked greedily at the huge collection of volumes. He noticed the writings of certain Roman authors, there were works by Tacitus, Seneca and Livy, there was Guillaume de Jumièges's famous Norman chronicle and the copy of the Gospels that Arnulphe had mentioned to him, covered in gold and precious stones, a gift from the monk Renauld at the time of William the Conqueror. There were so many works and parchments gathered in this place that the chevalier, dazzled, did not know where to look first.

The Precentor looked up when he heard him approaching. He was a flabby man with frog-like features and saggy cheeks and jowls. His protruding eyes were shaded by thick dark eyebrows and seemed to view the world disapprovingly. His black habit was held at the waist by a heavy leather strap from which a tablet and stylus hung.

Foulques flourished his hand over the volumes in the library for the chevalier's benefit and made a series of little movements with both his hands.

Galeran shook his head to say no. He was not familiar with the Benedictines' sign language, especially as these signs varied and meant different things from one religious order to another. In Cluny, for example, passing a finger from one eyebrow to another could just as easily mean a trout . . . as a woman!

Seeing that he had not been understood, the Precentor shrugged his shoulders even more disapprovingly. He snatched up his waxed tablet and etched the number 580 to tell the young man how many works there were in the library at Jumièges.

Even at Cluny, Galeran had never seen anything like it. The Bishop had not exaggerated, this abbey harboured a veritable treasure.

Still silent, Foulques then went and opened a small door at the end of the library and gestured expansively, inviting Galeran to go on past him. Galeran went into the holy of holies of the abbey, the famous scriptorium where the monks copied and illuminated manuscripts.

Despite the grey skies, the vaulted windows bounced the light from the cloisters off the whitewashed walls of the workshop. The room was larger than the library, and a pleasant smell of ink and wax hung in the air. A statue, sculpted from the trunk of an oak tree by one of the monks, represented Philibert, the founder of Jumièges. The monks had installed it at the end of the room, and there it stood, a silent and benevolent guardian.

Foulques had a team of ten transcribers working near the windows, sitting at their writing desks, bent over their work, with their pens scratching on the parchment.

On the other side of the room, he had put the novices on their stools, each with a board on his knees, preparing the vellum, cutting and cleaning the skins with pumice stone. Beyond, the older monks were carefully using an awl to pierce holes into the illuminated pages, and then binding them into volumes.

No one had turned to look. Just one young novice had dared to look up in amazement at the chevalier, for here, in the heart of the abbey, visitors were rare.

Foulques led Galeran over to a young monk who was hunched over his work illuminating a text.

Next to the desk, strange instruments were lined up on a small table: cornets of red and black ink, scalpels, styluses, goose and swan feathers in various sizes, chalk, plumblines . . .

Despite his youth, the monk was wielding his quill with great dexterity, tracing an interwoven design dotted with imaginary animals bearing disturbingly human expressions, and which were being devoured by crooked-shaped men.

Galeran heard the door open and looked up. Odon had just come in with a tall, sturdy monk. Both men's hands flew about in the air, making a series of signs that the chevalier was unable to interpret.

Odon noticed that Galeran was there, seemed to hesitate and then continued his mute conversation with Brother Onfroi, the abbey's cellarer.

The chevalier was affecting renewed interest in the transcriber's work when a novice rushed into the room. He was very young, probably only fifteen years old. He knelt down and grabbed the hem of Onfroi's robes and, slicing through the silence in the scriptorium, he cried shrilly: 'Father Abbot has asked me to fetch you, my Father, as well as Brother Odon of Lisieux and the Precentor. He is waiting for you in the chapter house, come straight away.'

Odon raised an astonished eyebrow, the Cellarer grimaced and the Precentor, becoming more disapproving by the minute, indicated to Galeran that he would have to leave him.

The monks went silently to the door, but Odon came over to the chevalier and shook his hand for some moments before falling in behind the others.

The chevalier felt a small piece of parchment between his

fingers and stowed it discreetly in his purse. He went straight back to his cell and there, sheltered from anyone's gaze, he unfolded the message that Odon had secretly handed him.

It was terse: 'Meet me by the jetty before the Sext service.'

Ever prudent, the monk had not even signed his name at the bottom of the parchment. Galeran, for his part, rolled it up into a little ball and swallowed it.

17

After the killing of the whale, and despite the approach of the equinox tides, navigation on the river was permitted again.

Small vessels with square sails made the most of the strong winds to go upriver along the Seine, tacking backwards and forwards. From time to time, heavy barges passed, grazing along the banks and laden with wood or cattle.

Galeran had sat down on an old tree stump not far from the jetty and was day-dreaming with his eyes half closed.

He looked up to find Odon emerging from a path lined with gnarled, twisted alders.

The monk was walking quickly and had an anxious expression on his face. Every trace of humour had abandoned his features, and he ran his hand nervously through his short red beard.

'So, Brother Odon, you have the deepest respect for the rule of silence, I did not hear you coming!' said the chevalier, getting to his feet.

The monk made do with nodding his head and muttered, 'Many thanks for waiting for me, my Lord.'

The two men spontaneously embraced each other and Galeran commented, 'You seem very serious, Brother.'

'Indeed, but first a question: what did you do with my message?'

'What one generally does with that sort of thing. Mind you, it was quite hard to swallow!'

Odon laughed quietly.

'I can see that we understand each other and that I can tell you more about the matter. Come over here, Chevalier, what I have to tell you is important and I want to make sure that no indiscreet ears pick up on our conversation.'

The monk led the chevalier towards a copse and sat down cross-legged in the grass, asking Galeran to sit down beside him.

'Here it is then, my Lord, but first a promise, what I am about to confide in you must remain between us.'

'It will be as you wish,' replied the chevalier seriously.

'My Bishop told me who you were and he disclosed to me his reason for getting you to come to Jumièges. You know that this abbey is one of the oldest bastions of our faith and, as such, deserves to be nurtured. For several months now, there have been complaints coming from here, alerting us to a relaxing of discipline and, worse still, of the Abbot's authority. In fact, the order of Saint Benoît is no longer being observed to the letter and this is sufficiently serious to justify my mission, *our* mission. You see, His Grace Arnulphe thought that, in addition to myself, there was a need for an independent visitor here, and he chose you.'

The chevalier shook his head angrily.

'You mean to say that Arnulphe engineered my trip to Lisieux with Bernard de Clairvaux? No, Odon, that won't hold water; if he took that sort of liberty on my account, then it is because there's something more serious afoot than a question of discipline and authority. Either way, I'm displeased with his methods and I will make a point of telling him so.'

'I understand, Chevalier, and I agree with you. Arnulphe must have had wind of something else, but what? He did not want to tell me anything more. And now that we are here, there are some very strange things happening, as if our arrival had set them off.'

'What sort of things?'

'Take this for a start, it is a missive from Arnulphe addressed to us. Probably a word of apology,' said the monk with a malicious smile.

The chevalier took the missive and slid it into his doublet.

'I'll read it later. Tell me what it is about.'

'Well, first of all, the complaint – as you've probably guessed – came from the Prior. Secondary rôles do not suit him, he wants to be first and he's got his eye on the Abbot's position. In my opinion it is nothing more than a power struggle, but I will have to look at the matter more closely; his accusations are too serious to ignore.'

Odon marked a few moments of silence, then he said in a

lowered voice, 'Another thing that complicates the matter is that the Abbot has a past . . .'

'What do you mean?'

'Oh, nothing specific. He took his orders very late in life, you know . . . before that he was married three times and widowed three times, almost straight away. What do you think of that?'

The chevalier pulled a face.

'A run of bad luck, like with dice!' he muttered. 'These things happen, but I imagine that the authorities looked into it?'

'Of course, of course, but it was not easy. The Abbot comes from a powerful family and there too, as with us, silence is the rule, but not for the right reasons!'

'So he withdrew from the world, renounced power and wealth . . . and yet, here he is again given a position of strength,' whispered the chevalier.

'Not since this morning,' said Odon calmly.

'What do you mean by that, my Brother?'

'This morning in the chapter the Abbot announced that his seal had disappeared. Now he's like a king without a crown.'

'The Abbot's personal seal or the abbey's seal?'

'Jumièges doesn't have a monastic seal, only the Abbot holds one. He uses it to sign the abbey's official acts and important letters.'

The chevalier nodded and then, separating each word to lend them greater gravity, he said, 'So, he can no longer certify any documents. I remember Bernard de Clairvaux telling me about a similar problem. His secretary had stolen his seal to put his signature on some of his personal letters. Are there any acquisitions of land or other transactions going on at the moment in Jumièges or in the region?'

'I know not, Chevalier, I had not thought of that,' replied Odon thoughtfully. 'I will find out. You're right, I had thought at first that it could only have been done to discredit the Abbot in my eyes, but this might stem from a still more dangerous manoeuvre which would involve the whole abbey.

'And that's not all. Listen to this: when the Abbot called us all together after the chapter this morning it was because something even more terrible had happened. Something which will pose a great problem for Jumièges at the time of the equinox tide.'

'What's that?'

'The relic of the founding saint, St Philibert's bone, has disappeared.'

'What's the connection with the tide?'

'There is to be a procession on the 21st of September, the day before the equinox. A procession in which the Abbot appeals to the patron saint of Jumièges to protect the village and the neighbouring hamlets because the high tide can have catastrophic consequences for them. On that day, the Abbot has to present St Philibert's bone to the inhabitants of the peninsula.'

'I see. Poor Abbot Eustache really does seem to be in a difficult position.'

'Oh, I agree with you there, my Lord. A bit too much so for my liking, as if someone were deliberately trying to discredit him.'

'How did the theft of the relic come about? I have visited the treasure chamber briefly and I seem to remember the guardian telling me that he was the only one who had the keys to it.'

'No, he *was* the only one to have the key that was on the old chain. But three days ago now the chain was found broken. The Abbot had it taken to the smith who could not get it finished before the festivities and he dropped it off in person this morning. And when they went down to the chamber, which is sealed by just one lock to which even the porter has a key, the two men realised that the relic of St Philibert had disappeared!'

'Strange coincidence, for the chain to be broken a few days before the theft . . .'

'That's not all, a young girl from the village, Edel, has disappeared too.'

'Edel . . . Yes, I seem to remember, a very comely maiden, I would even say a provocative one.'

'I do not know what she was like, but since dawn all the villagers have been searching for her. What's more, another damsel, young Mabille, was picked up in the early hours of the morning at the sanatorium. The nurse had to give her a poppy-draft she was so distressed. She seems to be prey to a great terror and has quite lost the power of speech.'

'Mabille? I met these two young girls at the feast. I think they were two rather dissimilar friends, as is often the case. The state of the one is perhaps not incompatible with the disappearance of the other. Odon, you're right, that makes quite a few puzzles and we've only been here since yesterday.'

'Yes, my Lord Galeran, and we won't be two too many to get to the bottom of it. You will have to help me find out who took the seal and the relic. The abbey's reputation is at stake. Perhaps the girl who disappeared has something to do with it all?'

'Perhaps, but I would be very surprised,' said the chevalier smiling. 'She's a pretty little thing who only thinks of manipulating her admirers. I would believe her to be guilty only of wanting to turn the heads of everyone in hose on the peninsula. As far as I can see, she's not thinking of much else. But we should not forget that that sort of girl often ends up running into trouble or meeting her match . . . So, anything is possible. Well and good, but there is another important fact.'

'What now?' asked Odon, anxiously.

'The death of poor Joce. He did not die like the fishermen.'

'Did he not drown?' exclaimed the young monk.

'Yes, but I am almost certain that his drowning was not an accident.'

'You mean that it was a crime, an assassination? Do you not think that would be a bit too much, chevalier. Must we see evil in everything?'

The chevalier's fine lips sketched a sad smile.

'Is that not our rôle, dear Odon, to explore every nook and cranny, to bring to light what lurks there, even if it hurts us?'

The young monk turned to the chevalier and contemplated the tall, wide forehead marked by a terrible scar, the resolute blue eyes and fine mouth, and he suddenly felt his fears dissolve.

''*De omnibus dubitandum est.*' Galeran added calmly.

'We must doubt everything,' repeated Odon. 'We are weak and we may not see the whole truth . . .'

'Nevertheless,' muttered the chevalier, 'we would know more if we could find out who rang the bell for Nocturn on Sunday night.'

'Are you jesting, Chevalier?'

'Nay, not at all,' replied Galeran.

'Explain yourself.'

'I discovered from Father Hosteller that it was usually Joce who rang in Nocturn, but I think that he was already dead by then.'

'That would mean that whoever rang in Nocturn instead of him was his assassin?'

'Yes . . . Or that they had noticed he'd disappeared. You must question the monks, Odon. There must be some detail that will shed light on this.'

'Very well,' sighed the monk. 'What will you do meanwhile?'

'Go to the pest-house and question the poor maiden. Then I will come back and see the Porter and old Sven; I still have a few questions for them.'

Odon nodded his head and, still staring at his companion's face, he said slowly: 'You are a strange man, Chevalier. Your perception is of a rare quality. Arnulphe knew what he was doing when he sent you here. Take care of yourself.'

'You too, Odon, and remember that now you are looking for a murderer!'

'Fie, so long as I'm just looking for him all is well!' retorted the monk and his mocking little smile reappeared.

18

'She has come back to her senses, my Lord. But you are no relation of hers?' asked the nurse as he led the chevalier through the corridors of the sanatorium.

'Why no, I am the guest of the Abbot Eustache and I happened to meet this child at the feast yesterday. She was with her young brother. She seemed happy and struck me as a naïve young girl. Where did you find her?'

'She came and knocked at the hatch and fainted in front of the door before we even opened it to her.'

'In your opinion, Father, has she been assaulted?' asked the chevalier.

'No, no, there was no disorder in her garments and she bore no trace of having been beaten.'

'Has she spoken since?'

'No, she has just wailed more pitifully than an animal, she seemed terribly frightened. I, therefore, thought it better to allow her a few hours of oblivion.'

'You did well, Father. And has she regained consciousness since then?'

'Yes, but she will not speak at all. She lies curled up on herself with her eyes closed. I have little idea what to do next, I assure you.'

'How do you know who she is if she does not speak, do you know her?'

'Nay, but one of the boys who works in the kitchens is a friend of her younger brother. He was in the courtyard when she was brought to the infirmary. I immediately sent word to the Abbot and to the little one's family.'

'Have her parents not come for her?'

'Oh yes, but given the state she is in, it seemed better for them to leave her here. They were in tears, the poor souls!'

'I see. Could you leave me alone with her, Father?'

'I will leave the door ajar and I'll wait for you in the corridor, Chevalier,' said the monk a little suspiciously.

'Thank you. Have no fear, Father, I wish her no ill, quite the contrary: I hope to be able to restore her to her former self.'

'May God help you, my Lord,' said the nurse, pushing open a little door. 'She is here, please go in.'

The cell was as dark and narrow as a corridor. It was stiflingly hot. Mabille lay wrapped in a heavy woollen blanket on a litter of straw, and the nurse had put a little brasier beside her.

The monk had spoken the truth. Lying on one side with her eyes closed, Mabille flicked her hands convulsively as if shooing away invisible demons. She did not seem to notice the chevalier.

Galeran took a stool and sat down without a word, looking at the young girl's sunken face beaded with acrid-smelling sweat. Then he put his hand gently on her forehead. It was burning hot.

'Mabille,' whispered the chevalier. 'It is I, Galeran de Lesneven, do not be afraid.'

The young girl did not react at all.

The chevalier stood up and moved the brasier aside abruptly. Next he went over to the narrow window and opened the shutter wide to let in the air. Then he called in the Friar Nurse:

'Father, your patient is suffocating. She must be allowed to breathe freely.'

'She was shivering, I was afraid she would catch cold! But what do you think, what should we do now?'

'Bring me some cool water and some linen cloths. We must bathe her forehead to clear her head . . . Do you have any black mustard, Father?'

'Yes, of course, for the treatment of chest pains!'

'Well in this case we're going to put it in a poultice on her feet to draw her blood down.'

'And if we do not succeed,' whispered the kindly monk, sorely vexed.

'Only faith can save, you should know that, Father,' said the chevalier with a laugh, 'Go on, quickly!'

The monk disappeared and came back shortly with what the chevalier had requested. Galeran uncovered the patient and wrapped her naked feet with the mustard poultice, while the nurse, averting his eyes discreetly, put a wet compress on her burning forehead.

'Now leave us,' ordered the chevalier curtly, exasperated by the man's fussing. 'I will call you as soon as she comes back to herself.'

Offended, the monk hesitated and then left, pulling the door to behind him.

Galeran came and sat back down at the head of the bed, anxiously watching the patient's reactions.

Her eyes opened abruptly. Now she looked around attentively.

She gave another plaintive sob and then said in a voice so weak that Galeran could barely hear it, 'Why am I here? It is daytime, why am I in bed?' She tried to sit up but let out a little scream: 'Oh, I remember, I remember!'

She fell back onto the bed and burst into tears.

Galeran sighed deeply. 'She is saved,' he thought.

He got up calmly, went to soak another cloth in the cool water and applied it gently to the young girl's forehead.

'You recognise me, do you not, Mabille?' said the chevalier, quietly.

The little creature turned her hazel eyes towards him but did not utter a word.

'My name is Galeran and do you remember, fair damsel, how we danced last night after the feast. We enjoyed ourselves.'

A small smile crept onto the young girl's face and she murmured: 'It is true, my Lord, it is true . . . we enjoyed ourselves.'

A fair time passed.

'I want to sit up, Chevalier,' she said suddenly. 'Could you help me up?'

Galeran held her under her arms and, lifting her forwards, helped her to lean back against the wall. Then he slid a cushion behind her head.

'And there was Edel, the lovely Edel you were so fond of,' he went on.

Hearing her friend's name, the brown eyes grew wide with terror and Mabille started sobbing again.

'Mabille, my little Mabille, have no fear, by my faith I will protect you,' said the chevalier seizing her hands and squeezing them in his own. He went on talking to her gently as if to a frightened infant.

'You mustn't be afraid any longer, little one.'

She sobbed all the louder and painstakingly articulated her friend's name.

'You know where she is, do you not?'

'The wolf,' sobbed Mabille, 'the green wolf . . .'

She tried to pull her hands away from his, she was so afraid that her teeth chattered. Drops of sweat mingled with her tears. Galeran, who was now sitting down beside her, held her firmly to him.

At last, she calmed down and let her head rest on the young man's shoulder. Her features, which had been distorted by her terror, seemed to relax a little. Sensing her fear receding, Galeran asked, 'Will you put your trust in me, Mabille? I will swear to protect you whatever happens. Look at me, please.'

The young girl looked up slowly and her terror-stricken eyes scrutinised the grave face that leant over her. Her breathing steadied gradually.

The chevalier waited without a word, letting her return slowly to her senses, allowing her to examine his face, then he called the nurse who was still listening behind the door, and he asked him for more water.

'Oh, she's back with us,' exclaimed the kind man. 'That's good, my child, I'll go straight away to fetch you some cold water.'

Touchingly happy, the monk turned quickly on his heel and made off at a run.

'There, we're alone now. Tell me what frightened you so much, fair damsel. Don't hide anything from me. It is Edel, is it not? Did you find her?'

'She's dead,' said Mabille in a tiny little voice. 'She was eaten by the wolf. I could not find her . . . It was because of the crows . . . The red veil . . .'

'What do you mean?' asked the chevalier, frowning. 'What red veil?'

'The bridal veil.'

'Was she married?'

The young girl gave no reply.

'Mabille, you must tell me everything, this is very serious. You mentioned a green wolf just now. Did you see a green wolf?'

'She was devoured by the green wolf, she was, I'm sure she was . . .'

The young girl was wringing her hands, getting into a state again. She started humming and singing while rocking backwards and forwards: *'Let's go, dear heart, the moon has arisen . . .'*

'Shush, shush, Mabille,' said the chevalier, worried by the young girl's distraction. 'Shush, everything's all right now, you're safe here. Tell me, where did you find your friend?'

'You're not to go there, Chevalier. The wolf will kill you too, and he'll eat your heart.'

'No, no, fair damsel, it takes more than a wolf, even a green one, to finish me off. I must find Edel, Mabille. If she is dead we must have her buried. You wouldn't want to leave your friend with no grave, would you?'

Mabille bit her lips and spoke in such a quiet voice that Galeran had to lean towards her.

'In the woods, right next to the pest-house. But I shan't go back there, I shan't!'

'No, Mabille, I'll go alone. Just tell me how I can find her body. I'll come back to see you this afternoon and if you feel a little stronger, I will take you home so that your parents can take care of you, I promise. Would you like that?'

The young man's deep, gentle voice and his eyes brimming with compassion took effect once again. The young girl calmed down and acquiesced with a timid nod of the head.

'Until then, stay here and do not talk to anyone about all this, do you hear? I myself will let the nurse and the Abbot of Jumièges know.'

Mabille nodded her head and explained in one breath, as if to be done with it, where and how she had found her friend's body.

19

Young Roderic had run all the way to the village and found it deserted. On the orders of the village elder, Drogtegand, every able-bodied man and woman was looking for young Edel. He crossed the square and stopped a moment to catch his breath. He let his stick fall to the ground and, bending over with his palms pressed against his knees, he fought for breath. He was about to get up when a sonorous voice spoke from behind him.

'I have found you at last, damn you.'

Roderic snatched up his stick and turned round slowly. Standing tall and imposing before him was Rurik the Dane. The young groom jumped in surprise when he saw how the whale-killer had changed.

His leather hunting cape spattered with mud, his hair wildly awry and a heavy axe in his hand, the Dane's mouth was twisted with rage and his eyes, normally so distant, blazed fiercely.

Roderic instinctively took a step back and then, holding his stick with both hands, he took up a stance in front of Rurik with his legs spread apart.

'What do you want from me, Dane, and what gives you the right to speak to me like that?'

'You touched my wife, you vermin, you dared to touch her with your filthy paws.'

'What are you saying? You've had too much to drink, Dane. Your wife! I did not even know that you were married, and who is it that you've married, what's her name?'

'Edel, my Edel!' wailed the Dane as he dropped his axe and, lowering his head, stormed forward towards the groom.

The two men rolled in the dust. Hearing the name of his betrothed, Roderic was overwhelmed with rage and managed to free himself. He was winded but was able to strike a mighty blow with his two fists knotted together onto the back of Rurik's neck as he came up. The Dane fell back to his knees, breathing hard.

Some of the old folk of the village who were crossing the main square cried out when they saw the two men fighting. One of their number, an old friend of Roderic's father, the porter, gamely tried to stand between them, putting his hand onto the Dane's shoulder in a peaceful gesture. Rurik brushed him aside furiously, straightened himself and, as the old boy was coming back towards him, sent him sprawling on the ground with a tremendous punch.

Seeing this, the others forgot their infirmity and ran off to find help.

Making the most of the diversion created by the old man, Roderic threw himself at the Dane again, striking him furiously in the ribs with his head. A blow like that would have thrown anyone other than Rurik off balance, but he barely wavered before turning to face the young groom again.

Roderic quickly realised that he would have no chance at all in hand to hand combat. The sheer stature and the training of this whale-hunter made him a fearful adversary. The two men, hunched, their legs well apart, circled warily, breathing noisily.

Even though he had the advantage of size and weight, the Dane was getting angry and was breathing more and more heavily. The young groom evaded his blows, and slipped under his guard to strike him in the groin.

After a few minutes the two fighters moved away from each other, glowering with hate.

Roderic was very pale and he was holding his nose which spewed blood. A vigorous head-butt from the Dane had broken it. Rurik, on the other hand, had one eye that was half closed and the line of his brow was very swollen.

'I challenge you to a fight to the death,' growled the Dane pushing back the young man who had taken up his stick, 'not some child's squabble. Where I come from, dishonour can only be washed with blood. You spilt my wife's blood by possessing her, I will spill yours by cutting your throat!'

'Dishonour,' roared Roderic furiously. 'Edel is my betrothed and not your wife, and you dare to talk of dishonour!'

'And yet I did marry her last night, your Edel, and with her consent,' retorted the Dane.

'You lie!' growled the young man, strangled with rage, 'you lie, no one from these parts would have married you to my Edel.'

'If you get out of this alive you can go and ask the priest. He'll tell you Rurik's not lying. What weapon do you choose, groom boy?'

The young man hesitated, he was hardly adroit at handling arms but imagining Edel in the Viking's arms was suddenly unbearable to him! Rurik must be lying, it was not possible that she had consented to marry him. And yet, he remembered the festivities and the way she had been making eyes at this barbarian!

'The axe!' he cried, his heart filled with rage.

'I accept,' said the Dane. 'You have chosen a man's weapon. Before one of us dies, admit that you sullied my wife.'

'No one has ever possessed Edel, you dog, she's my intended. She's a virgin, pure as the moon. You have no right to think otherwise. I'll see that you pay for these words and for all the others!'

The young man's spirit made the Dane hesitate. There was too much sincerity in his conviction.

'You never touched her, will you swear on Christ Jesus?'

This was too much for Roderic who picked up the stick which he had thrown to the ground and struck a terrible blow at the Dane. This time the big man did not have time to duck, but he merely shook his head as if the stick had barely brushed past him before leaping at the groom, grabbing him by the belt and lifting him over his head as if he were a child.

'Put him down,' said a deep voice.

Surrounded by a dozen or so men armed with lances and pitchforks, the village elder, Drogtegand, stood a few paces from the two fighting men.

Rurik hesitated and then slowly put his adversary back on the ground. Roderic took a few paces back and turned to face the villagers.

'Leave us,' said Rurik. 'This is between me and him, men's business.'

'No, Dane, you are here within my jurisdiction and Roderic is in my right,' replied old Drogtegand calmly.

'Wise Drogtegand,' interrupted Roderic, 'for once this evil-doing Dane is right, I have a quarrel to settle with him, and I need nothing more than God's help in this fight.'

'Well, Roderic, if quarrel there is, it is I who shall settle it and I shall bring judgement as is the custom. God would surely approve of that.'

Drogtegand's tone was implacable, Roderic wanted to protest but one look at the old man's determined face was enough to persuade him that it would be pointless.

Dressed in a long robe of off-white cloth, the elder stood head and shoulders above the others. No one knew his age, but it was known that he had survived many generations and that he knew the secrets of the past.

Yet he was still as agile as a youth. His beard and his long hair were honey-coloured, his face was leathery and his slanting eyes always seemed to be gazing into the distance. Some said that he had the benign powers of the ancient Druids; people talked about it as far afield as Caudebec and even, they said, in the town of Rouen. They had lost count of the sick that he had cured just by laying his strong hands on them. Drogtegand had the gift. For the villagers it was sacrilegious to contradict him.

Drogtegand could have become a monk, so wholly were his actions governed by wisdom and faith, but he had chosen to live amongst the people. The woman he had loved had died in childbirth and he had never married again, devoting himself and his goodness to others. The monks themselves consulted him when they had problems with the villagers, or when they did not know how to settle the conflicts between neighbouring lords.

'Follow me, both of you, we must speak,' said the old man severely.

Rurik hesitated. Should he leave or obey this patriarch whom he respected?

Fate decided for him.

Shouts and cries were heard from above the village. A little group made up of monks and foresters arrived in the square carrying a stretcher. The men's faces were strained. The women who had joined the cortège had tears glistening in their eyes. Galeran led them, tall and rigidly upright.

Old Drogtegand immediately noticed the chevalier's sombre expression, then he looked over at the litter, on which he could make out a small human form covered with a blanket.

Roderic was as pale as a corpse. The Dane, too, was staring at the litter which the men had laid down at the elder's feet.

The chevalier came over to the patriarch and stopped a few paces from him, greeting him with a respectful tilt of the head. The crowd in the square was becoming bigger, people were running to see what was going on. Despite the cuffs distributed freely by their mothers, inquisitive children managed to squeeze to the front.

Everyone was talking at once.

The elder raised his hand.

'Peace, my friends,' he said in a loud voice and, as if by magic, the great square fell silent.

Then the old man turned towards Galeran and returned his greeting.

'I am the elder of the village, my name is Drogtegand, my Lord Chevalier.'

'My name is Galeran de Lesneven and I have been the guest of the Abbot Eustache these last days. I found the lifeless body of this young girl not far from the pest-house. The nurse, who is here present, identified her as the young Edel . . . I believe the people of your village were looking for her.'

At the sound of Edel's name, a heartrending cry rang out. Roderic scattered the people in his path and threw himself at the litter. The chevalier grabbed him just as he was about to lift up the blanket which covered the frail silhouette.

'No, Roderic, not now!'

The chevalier's voice was curt. Drogtegand turned to Galeran and asked simply:

'My Lord, do you not think it would be better for us to discuss this under my roof? I was going to ask Roderic and the Dane to follow me to settle their differences there. But where has he gone?'

Making the most of the commotion and the distraction of the locals, Rurik had disappeared.

'You, you and you, find the Dane for me and bring him back alive,' the old man ordered three stout youths armed with lances. 'Follow me, Chevalier, if you please. You others, take the litter. Roderic, come with us, my boy.'

20

The elder waited for everyone to find some sort of place for themselves, in the low-ceilinged room, before he spoke. He gazed abstractly over the men gathered there; the women and children had been excluded and remained outside.

Roderic's distraught face never wavered from the shape lying on the litter, and the torment he was experiencing could be read in his blood-shot eyes.

With his tunic covered in dust, his nose oozing blood and his face so deathly pale, even his own father would have trouble recognising him, Drogtegand thought sadly.

The chevalier had remained standing. The elder looked at him for a while before turning to the nurse who had dropped heavily onto a bench. In the centre of this circle of men the litter rested on a pair of makeshift trestles.

On Drogtegand's orders, two armed men took up posts on either side of the door which stood wide open. The old man did not intend to be disturbed but would never have agreed to close his door. He said that like this he could hear the inhabitants of the village breathing, even at night.

Drogtegand sat down on a stool: 'We are listening, my Lord Chevalier. But first, a question. Have you alerted Abbot Eustache?'

'Yes, the Friar Nurse sent one of his novices to tell him that we were coming to you and that it would be advisable for him to join us. I would, nevertheless, like to inform you of several things before he arrives.'

'I'm listening.'

'First of all, I would like you to look at this,' said the chevalier, as he slowly drew the blanket back from poor Edel's body.

The reactions were very varied. The Friar Nurse who had already seen the carnage, instinctively lowered his eyes, so appalling was the spectacle to behold.

Roderic sighed feebly before slipping to the floor, unconscious. With Galeran's help, the nurse carried him to Drogtegand's bed.

As for the patriarch, he came up to the mutilated body and examined it in detail.

'Well,' he said after some time, 'I have never seen anything like it before. It looks as if, even in such a short space of time, this poor child's body has been well and truly ravaged by the creatures of the forest.'

Drogtegand turned to Galeran.

'According to hearsay from one of the servant boys at the infirmary, my Lord Chevalier, you are a man of great knowledge. What do you make of it?'

Galeran was thinking, staring all the while at the body, and he eventually said calmly: 'We must make a distinction between the damage done by the scavengers and birds of prey, and whatever it was that really brought about this child's death.'

Rumbles of protest immediately sprang up around the room. The patriarch raised an appeasing hand and asked for silence once more:

'If I have understood you correctly, my Lord, you're implying that this was not just a simple accident?'

'That is what I believe,' said Galeran forcefully. 'This was murder!'

This time there was no calming the gathering, everyone seemed to be outraged.

'No predator,' the chevalier continued, 'not even a rabid wolf would, in my opinion, be capable of causing the damage that we see here. No one could open the chest so cleanly nor, as it appears, in one go, nor could they remove the vital organs with such precision!'

'I noticed that too,' said Drogtegand in a level voice. 'Besides, in high summer wolves do not prey on people, not when there's so much game for them to eat.'

The old man covered Edel up again, made an expansive sign of the cross over her body, and then went to sit back down, muttering: 'We are, therefore, dealing with a human predator . . .'

The chevalier came over to him: 'What is the green wolf?' he asked abruptly.

'Oh! You've heard of that! A childling's legend, nothing more, and also an excuse for the local men to celebrate the feast day of Saint John.'

'I'm listening, Drogtegand.'

'This custom dates back a very long way. There have always been a lot of wolves in the region of the Terre Gémétique. Saint Philibert, who founded the abbey, and Saint Austreberthe, each had their own way of taming them. That is where the legend stems from. Since then, people have said that the wolves have some sort of allegiance to the abbey and no longer kill people for meat.'

'Why a green wolf?'

'I know not, probably because it is a colour associated with bad luck.'

'Does green not symbolise fate rather than bad luck?' asked Galeran. 'As on the green meadow of ordeals – on a background of this colour good or evil emerges.'

'Perhaps you are right, Chevalier, I had not thought of green in this way,' said the elder, nodding slowly.

'You said it was a children's fable?'

'Yes, a fairy tale, although perhaps one that's only used when they're refusing to eat their gruel. 'Eat up or the green wolf will eat you up!' There are no ogres or dragons here, there's the green wolf!'

The tall old man paused for a moment before continuing. Galeran did not take his eyes off him.

'You know that Saint John's day coincides with the summer solstice. It is an important time for the men, harbinger of the harvests and the last important jobs to be done before the winter. It is then that our villagers here like to celebrate the green wolf, the wolf that was tamed by Saint Philibert himself. During the course of the festivities they choose a man to represent it.'

'A man?'

'Yes, every year the villagers select a new green wolf. He is a simple peasant like themselves and he fulfils the rôle until the following summer solstice. There has never been the same wolf twice, they say.'

'Do the wolves have a special costume?'

'Why yes, they are dressed in a green capuchon, their faces hidden by the hood which is topped with a stuffed wolf's head. This costume has been passed from wolf to wolf for a very long time, and it frightens the children. The wolf is always someone from Conihout, where the abbey has its vineyards.'

'Oh, and why is that then?' Galeran asked.

'I confess that I do not know, my Lord,' Drogtegand admitted humbly, and Galeran continued.

'And what form does this strange election take?'

'Strange is the word. Led by the old wolf, the villagers ring bells as they process to the abbey where they are blessed by the Reverend Father and where they attend a mass. Then the procession moves off towards the wolf's clearing. There they have a huge fire and they dance round the fire.'

'*Let's go, dear heart, the moon has arisen,*' Galaran murmured, repeating the words he had heard Mabille intoning.

'That's it, those are the words of Saint John's canon. The locals sing it round the fire and it is then that they choose the new green wolf.'

The old man seemed to be reliving the strange custom. His breath whistled as he continued his description.

'As the flames lick the sky, the old wolf and the last man in the *farandole* have to catch the elected wolf three times. The others can close in the circle but must not lay a hand on him. They throw him a club for him to defend himself, and he defends himself like the very devil, hitting, leaping, trying to escape the *farandole* around him. Men are brought down with gashes to their heads and their faces, streaming with blood. They are replaced by others. The circle is broken and reformed and in the end there is a terrible scramble. They grab him and carry him towards the fire to throw him onto it . . . But it is just an act and the celebrations go on for another four days after that.'

'Well,' said the chevalier, 'that's quite a manly pastime! Who then was elected three months ago?'

'Young Jendeus, and it has hardly brought him good luck. He had an accident shortly afterwards and has been recuperating at the abbey ever since. They say he's dying.'

'What sort of accident?' asked Galeran, visibly interested.

'I never knew. The Abbot had him segregated straight away and even his family could not visit him. You will have to ask him.'

'Many thanks for your words, Drogtegand. They have enlightened me. And yet none of this tells us what really happened to poor Edel. And the Abbot still is not here . . .'

A groan made them turn round, Roderic was regaining consciousness. He tried to stand up and eventually sat on one of the benches.

Even though he was still very pale, he just managed to say: 'We must find Rurik.'

'Yes, my boy,' the elder said calmly, 'but, given what has happened, I think your differences can wait.'

'Our differences as you call them, Drogtegand, lie there on that litter. It is my Edel, and that savage has massacred her!' replied Roderic shrilly.

Galeran went over to the young man and put a hand on his shoulder:

'Explain yourself, Roderic.'

'He was looking for me to kill me. The animal dared to say that Edel was his wife and that . . .'

'And that?' insisted the chevalier.

'And that she was no longer a virgin,' whispered the young man. 'He dared to say that I had soiled her, me, her intended! He's the one that killed her. He said that in his country, an insult like that was paid for with blood. And Edel, look what he's done to her!' sobbed the young man, putting his head into his hands.

'What, pray, is going on here?'

The Abbot had just come into the cottage, followed by the Prior and Brother Odon. After glancing quickly round the room, he went over to the litter.

'You called for me, Drogtegand, and you, Chevalier? Who has died?' he said, lifting the cover before the chevalier could stop him.

Eustache paled and stepped back, crossing himself. The Prior looked without blinking and then ran out, leaning forward. The men heard him vomiting close to the door.

'Who did this?' muttered Eustache, indicating poor Edel's body.

'A wolf – animal or human,' replied the chevalier gravely.

'Do you mean to say that a man, a creature of God, could have done this?' said the Abbot. 'But this girl has been devoured!'

'The world is vast and diverse,' interceded Brother Odon. 'Like myself, my Lord Abbot, you would have no job in life if all God's creatures always stayed quietly in His bosom.'

'And if it was a werewolf?' asked the Prior who had just come back into the cottage, his habit dirtied by long yellowish streaks. 'Some damned soul marked by the Beast.'

The Abbot paled and went to sit down at the other end of the room, he looked old and tired. Noticing this, Drogtegand sensibly decided to close the session.

'Yes,' said Eustache with obvious relief. 'I must get back to the abbey. Once she has been cleaned and prepared, have this poor child brought to the church of Notre-Dame. We will say Mass, asking that her soul might rest in peace before we bury her. Ask the sisters in the village to take care of her.'

'It will be done as you wish, Father,' Drogtegand acquiesced, immediately giving the relevant orders.

The death knell rang out in the village then and was soon relayed by the two churches of the great abbey.

When the men came out of the cottage they saw that the rays of sunlight were ringed with red and that heavy clouds were billowing up from the coast. The twigs and the dust on the little roadways between the houses were swept along by gusts of wind.

The anxious crowd dispersed into groups talking in lowered tones, and Drogtegand ordered the last few onlookers to go home. The council of elders would meet later in the evening after the funeral service, he told them.

The chevalier asked Brother Odon whether he would accompany him to the pest-house. He had promised Mabille that he would accompany her to the village and he was now wondering whether it would not be better to leave her where she was – quite safe with the monks in the infirmary.

This whole business was of great concern to him. Rurik the Dane had fled, the relic and the seal had disappeared, there had already been two deaths over and above the unfortunate fishermen, and somewhere, a man capable of ripping a woman's heart out was still at large . . .

With a deep sigh, the chevalier looked up at the high walls of the abbey.

'*De omnibus dubitandum est!*' said a quiet, slightly mocking voice. 'We must doubt everything, Galeran, it was you who taught me that!'

Galeran caught Odon's eye as he walked along beside him. And suddenly, as if in response to the terrible tension that weighed on them, the two men burst out laughing.

PART THREE

'He loveth righteousness and judgement:
the earth is full of the goodness
    of the Lord.'

Psalm 33, verse 5

21

The chevalier closed the door of the cell again, and hung his waterproof leather cape on a nail. After a brief glance round, he sat down on his mattress, took from his purse the parchment that Odon had given him and, by the light of the night lamp, he deciphered the Bishop of Lisieux's fine hand-writing.

According to Arnulphe, the *circatores* – the 'investigators', monks who spied on their brothers – had been sending him alarming reports about Jumièges for nearly a year. One of them, who he could not name and who had persuaded Arnulphe to take action, had told him of a transaction that was being effected concerning the sale of a relic, a sale that was to all intents and purposes being conducted by the Abbot himself!

When he had read it, Galeran put the parchment into the flame and made sure that it was entirely consumed. He stood up briskly and went over to the window. The darkness outside was opaque, impenetrable. He scattered the few remaining ashes in the wind and then went back to his mattress and lay down, fully clothed.

As he stared at the shadows that danced across the beams in the ceiling, he tried to remember every last detail of what had been a horribly eventful day.

First of all Mabille . . . . As he had promised on his first visit, he had returned to the sanatorium with Brother Odon. An unpleasant surprise awaited the two men.

They found the girl sitting on her bed, leaning against the wall with her frail arms hugging her knees to her chest. She was wild-eyed and was muttering something as if she were asleep; then, seeming to wake up, she started screaming so shrilly it made their blood run cold. When anyone spoke to her she fell straight back into her state of prostration. Galeran did not know what to think, he nodded briefly to Odon and the two men left the bed-chamber, leaving Mabille to her delirium and to the care of the stalwart monks.

Abbot Eustache had been to see her in the early afternoon with some of his officials, and had been so moved by her condition that he had given the order that she should be tended at the sanatorium until she recovered. He had arranged for a pious widow – who had withdrawn from the village and now lived in a nearby hermitage – to watch over the girl.

Following directions from the porter at the sanatorium, Galeran and his companion had then made their way to the young Dane's cottage. As the chevalier had expected, Rurik's den was empty. The man was well and truly a fugitive.

And so they had searched the single room from top to bottom. The state of the bed, with its ripped mattress and torn blankets, suggested a desperate struggle rather than the ardours of lovemaking. The chevalier remembered what young Roderic had said.

Had the Dane not publicly accused Edel of tricking him, had he not revealed that she was not a virgin bride? The exchange between the two young lovers must have been heated indeed, and Galeran remembered the characteristic bruises on the dead girl's cheeks . . . Had the Dane inflicted this punishment on his unfaithful bride, and had she fled in terror?

Under the bed, Galeran had found one of the cherry red ribbons that Edel had worn in her hair on the evening of the revelries.

'Pretty little Edel who had dreamed of the distant Orient ever since she seduced her young Nordic god. Perhaps, like so many Normans, he had hoped to join Roger II in Sicily and to conquer some fiefdom beyond the Mediterranean,' thought the chevalier, sadly contemplating the little red ribbon now covered in dust . . . 'Edel, leaping and happy, Edel who probably thought she was immortal, just because she so loved life . . . and because she had not even reached her twentieth year!'

Tight-lipped, the chevalier had carried on with his minute search and had to yield to the evidence. There was no trace of blood in the house and, what was more, he found it difficult to imagine the Dane dragging the girl outside to cleave her in two out in the forest. No, he might have killed her with a single blow or might even have strangled her, but would not have tortured her thus and torn out her heart.

But why had he refused to explain himself and why had he disappeared? What exactly did he know? Did he feel that he was in some way threatened?

The injuries inflicted on the young girl had prompted the chevalier to thinking that the unfortunate creature had been the victim of some horrible ritual. But then he considered Edel's character. Whether one liked it or not, she had been a shameless girl who had a taste for lies and secrets, she had been arrogant. Had she pitilessly broken some man's heart or wounded his pride – and had whoever that was consummated his vengeance in this monstrous way? Because there might be any number of other men who should not be ruled out of this affair.

Roderic, of course, the cuckolded intended . . . but others too, perhaps, others that were as yet unknown. Perhaps whoever had deflowered her, and from whom she must have been hiding when she married the Dane in secret. And then there was the Sexton, who eyed her longingly during the dance, and those other men she had inflamed without ever actually promising them anything. There were many men who could have been driven to murder by Edel's provocations, very many, too many!

As he looked round the weed-ridden vegetable patch, Brother Odon had found strange marks along the walls of the cottage. Deep imprints of knees and hands in the soft soil in front of the only window, as if someone had waited there on all fours for a long time. Someone who had possibly watched the two lovers, unbeknown to them . . .

His neck stiff, Galeran turned towards the wall of the cell, trying to find the best position in which to sleep. The hooting of an owl made him jump and, as sleep evaded him still, images of the terrible day unfolded again in his mind.

Now he saw the little clearing that poor Mabille had described to him in a moment of lucidity . . . the crows leaving their booty with angry cries, the mutilated corpse behind the dense shrubs. He had found no footprints around it, but he had noticed that a patch of grass looked almost bruised, as if a herd of deer had jostled and stampeded over it.

The silence that hung heavily over the scene had seemed somehow supernatural to him. At one point he had almost thought he heard a sort of muffled cackling coming from the thicket, and he had noticed that the men with him were nervous and frightened too.

To add to their ill-fortune, one of them, drawn on by the smell, had stumbled across the rotting carcass of a large billy goat. This macabre find had terrified the humble peasant and the others had said, through gritted teeth, that it was time to leave. There must have been something truly evil at the bottom of this!

The chevalier had had to put Edel's body onto the make-shift stretcher himself, because the men had looked at it in such horror and had not wanted to go near it. Eventually, the anxious little troop had set off back to the village.

As they walked, the chevalier was struck again and again by the same thought: Who would have dared to do this?

When all was said and done, why could it not have been a chance encounter, a murderous, travelling stranger who might cross your path by chance one day on the edge of the woods! A demon, a rabid madman; a werewolf, the Prior had said and these words reminded the chevalier of the crooked silhouette that he had glimpsed that first evening as he went home from the revelries.

In some ways, perhaps Prior Angilbert was right, this criminal was more like an animal than a human being!

Galeran remembered a story that his father Gilduin had told him some years earlier.

One of their villeins, a good man that everyone liked, had been bitten by his dog. The animal had run off and the man had tried in vain to track him down.

According to one of his friends, the wound was terrible and made him suffer grievously. Several days later the man was in a pitiable state. He had started foaming at the mouth and grinding his teeth, and he growled like an animal. The terrified villagers had tried to catch him to tie him up but the man, as if possessed of superhuman strength, had managed to escape after injuring three of his assailants. The following morning, the villagers had found two cows with their bellies ripped open.

Furious, they armed themselves with axes and pitchforks, and set off in pursuit of the rabid man.

Gilduin de Lesneven had arrived too late to save him. The villagers, terrified by his metamorphosis, had put him to death like a savage beast, pinning him to the farmhouse door with a pitchfork . . . But several amongst them, touched by the same murderous delirium, had already fled in their turn.

The chevalier turned over on his bed, and punched his horse-hair pillow. With heavy eyelids, he sat up abruptly, thinking he heard a creak behind his door.

But no, there was nothing there. His usual difficulty sleeping had only ever been aggravated during his stays in various monasteries. Often the bell-ringing, the chanting and the monks' busy footsteps in the corridors would keep him awake until dawn. It has to be said that not long after midnight struck the bells seemed to swing into action for Nocturn, then the monks would go back to bed until Matins in the 'witching' hours pre-dawn and finally, after a brief sleep, they would rise once more, with the sun this time, for Prime. It was difficult to get to sleep in these circumstances.

Not without some emotion did Galeran remember the words of his friend Abbot Huon when he had asked him why there were so many services at night: 'It is true that we choose the dark hours, my friend. But, after all, someone has to watch over the world while people are asleep. It is our duty. During the hours of night our prayers spread over you like a shield.'

These words had been carved into the young man's mind. From then on, whenever fate turned against him, he liked to imagine this shield of prayer protecting him at night.

By a circuitous sequence of thoughts, he came to remember his knight's oath, that moment when, aged fifteen, he had sworn on his sword before his peers.

"Omnipotent father . . . thou who hast allowed on this earth that the sword be used to repress the wrong-doings of Evil and to defend the course of Justice, thou who hath instituted the order of chivalry in order to protect thy people . . . Let my heart be so disposed to the good that I may be thy servant and may never abuse this sword, no,

nor any other, to injure any person unjustly, but that I may use it always to defend what is Just and Right."'

As he turned over in bed again, he told himself that the Bishop had entrusted him with a truly ugly affair. Finally, his weariness overcame him and he succumbed to sleep.

22

Galeran woke with a start. He thought he had heard someone cry out. He sat up in bed and wiped his brow which was beaded with sweat.

It had not been a dream, he really had heard a scream and then silence had fallen again. All he could distinguish now was a sort of distant murmur and that could easily have been a sound made by the gusts of wind in the tall trees.

The chevalier rose to his feet and, swinging open his shutter, looked out of the narrow window onto the abbey gardens. Dawn had not yet broken, and only the ghostly silhouettes of the whitewashed tree trunks in the orchard stood out in the dark.

The sound of quiet footsteps made him turn round. It was coming from the corridor. No longer hesitating, he snatched up his dagger and silently opened the door of his cell.

The torches along the walls had been extinguished, leaving the corridor in shadow. Nothing moved. Slipping his weapon into his belt, the chevalier gently pulled the door to and put his palm against the wall to guide himself. He could still hear a vague murmuring. It was not the wind but definitely muffled voices and they seemed to be coming from the infirmary.

A feeble glimmer of light filtered under the door. The chevalier heard a moan of pain accompanied by the sound of furniture being knocked over, and then quiet sobbing like the whimpering of an injured animal.

Just as Galeran was about to put his hand on the latch, the door opened slightly and the Hosteller slipped out with a look of grave concern on his face. He was a tall man and he jumped in surprise when he saw the young chevalier's silhouette, raising his lantern well up above his head.

'Who goes there? Oh, it is you, Chevalier, you frightened me,' exclaimed Father Baudri, rapidly pulling the door closed behind him. 'What are you doing here in the dark like this?'

'I thought I heard someone screaming, Father,' replied the chevalier. 'I wanted to know what was going on and whether I could be of any help to you.'

'Your ears did not deceive you, my son. It is a poor soul in a piteous state that we have taken to the infirmary. Nothing too serious, though, you should return to your cot. The Friar Nurse and the Sexton are looking after him. Our Abbot himself has come to help him.'

'What's the matter with the poor man, is it one of the monks or a pilgrim?' asked the young man. 'Believe me, if there is anything I can do to help . . .'

'Oh, really no!' the monk retorted abruptly, putting his heavy hand authoritatively on the chevalier's shoulder. It would be better to go back to sleep, my Lord. As for what's wrong with him, I'm just a hosteller not a seer. And it is better that way. I will light your way back to your cell.'

The chevalier, sensing that it would be out of place to insist, thanked the Hosteller and retraced his steps to the door of his cell accompanied by the older man.

23

Inside the infirmary everything was now silent and the monks were waiting.

'They've gone. May we proceed, Reverend Father?' whispered the nurse uncomfortably.

Abbot Eustache was very pale as he turned towards him. His hands were shaking a little as he replied quietly:

'Come on, Brother, we have lost too much time.'

'Look, he is quieter now,' said the monk, making his way to the back of the infirmary where the weak light of a single candle revealed two silhouettes bound closely together.

A tall solid youth, wearing only a torn tunic, was being held in a firm grip by the Sexton. He was glowering at them in bewilderment.

Avoiding any abrupt movements, the nurse went over to him slowly. The young man rolled his eyes in terror and tried to move away. He was grinding his teeth and foaming at the mouth as if he were afflicted with epilepsy.

'Calm down, Jendeus, calm down, we do not mean you any harm. We want to help you, do you understand,' the friar nurse was saying.

The man did not seem to understand. He formed his mouth into a circle as if to speak and a stifled, animal groan came out.

'Hold him firm, Brother Gachelin. Reverend Father, would you come over, pray, I'd like to show you something.'

The Abbot nodded and came over to the Friar Nurse.

'You see, look,' whispered the latter, firmly grasping Jendeus's wrist.

An ugly wound which oozed pus ran across the back of the poor man's hand and onto his swollen and blackened fingers.

'Do you see, Reverend Father, that is where the fox bit him. The evil humours are still there. And then look at this.'

Turning the injured hand over, the monk pointed out a burn

that had imprinted a shape at the base of Jendeus's thumb. It was a strange shape, rather like a key . . .

'His brother applied Saint Hubert's iron to him here. But he did not know how to go about it, either the iron was not hot enough, or the key did not draw blood. It has given him some respite, but . . .'

'. . . the evil is still there,' breathed the Abbot. 'The black blood has spread through him. If only I had made the decision to cut him rather than leaving him in the hostelry in the hopes that we just had to wait for the evil to release him.'

'What are you saying, Reverend Father?'

'When I think of that poor young maiden, I wonder . . .'

'Do you think that Jendeus could have killed her?' exclaimed the Friar Nurse. 'It is impossible, he was at the hostelry and we tied him to his cot, you know very well.'

'Oh, I know not, I know not, my brother. But do you see any other explanation for the unhappy girl's terrible wounds? Even the Prior was moved to mention the word werewolf when he saw the body . . . and then of course there are the stories of the green wolf!'

'Forgive me, Reverend Father,' interrupted the Sexton.

'What is it?'

'I do not believe that this poor devil is guilty. Even if we were to believe that he committed the crime, can you really see him coming meekly back to his cot here? He would have disappeared and gone back to join his brother wolves far off in the forests.'

The Abbot gave no reply, he could not control the slight trembling in his hands. After a long pause, he announced: 'Your observations seem sensible to me, Brother Gachelin, and yet . . . I cannot think of any other possible culprit but poor Jendeus.'

The Reverend breathed deeply and then continued, hammering out each syllable: 'I do not want to think of any other, because he is the only one who might be forgiven!'

The two monks nodded. Jendeus was watching them, motionless, a fine white foam flecking his lips.

'Come on, my brothers,' rallied the Reverend, 'we have waited too long. May God help us and may Saint Hubert guide our every move.'

'Reverend Father, I shall need your help, you must slip the thread from the sacred stole over his forehead. Brother Gachelin, sit him down on this stool and hold him firmly.'

The nurse went over to a leather chest, opened it and took out something that was wrapped in white linen. He came back over to them as he unwound the material to reveal the highly-sharpened blade of a knife.

'Reverend Father, do you have the sacred white thread?'

'Yes, Brother,' replied the Abbot, and added more quietly, 'I am ready.'

'I too,' said Gachelin.

The nurse heaved a great sigh and came up to Jendeus who did not seem to have seen the blade.

The monk grabbed the skin of his forehead and stretched it before making an incision in the shape of a cross. Scarlet blood sprang from the cleaved flesh. Jendeus shrieked and tried to struggle free from the Sexton's embrace.

Despite his cries, the Abbot leant over him and slipped the fine white thread from the stole of Saint Hubert into the wound, making the sign of the cross.

The nurse gently released the skin of the forehead which closed over the tiny scrap of sacred cloth.

Jendeus was moaning and rocking backwards and forwards, his face streaming with blood.

'The evil humours are leaving, Father,' said the nurse.

'May God hear you, my son,' replied the Abbot making the sign of the cross. 'Keep him in this room for nine days as is the custom. I will see him again when he is "released", and I will hear his confession then. Until then, I entrust him to you, to the exclusion of all your other responsibilities.'

'Very good, Reverend Father. It shall be done as you have commanded.'

The Abbot nodded a brief farewell to the Sexton and, after a last look at Jendeus, he left the room.

The nurse grabbed a piece of cloth which he soaked in a basin of clear water, and he carefully cleaned the reddened wound before binding Jendeus's forehead with a length of white linen.

Jendeus had been 'cut', from now on his blood would carry

the celestial breath, which would beat back the black blood of the beast. His eyelids were closed and his body seemed to be relaxing gradually.

24

That morning wise Drogtegand woke with his heart full of bile.

For the first time since the death of Abbot Guillaume in 1142, the meeting of the council of elders, which had taken place the previous evening, had been turbulent and riotous. In truth, neither Drogtegand nor his five fellow wise elders had succeeded in making the furious villagers see sense.

The old man came out of his cottage and, pulling on his long warm cloak, he sat down on a block of wood in front of his door and looked round bitterly.

Chickens were scratching for food between the houses. Seagulls were wheeling silently above the abbey. The village was incredibly peaceful, especially since the great equinoctial storms and their cortège of destruction were expected in two days' time.

Drogtegand screwed up his eyes into slits. A group of pilgrims in long brown cloaks was making its way up to the abbey along the white track. The procession for Saint Philibert, which was due to take place the following day before Terce, was already drawing visitors over to the peninsula.

Armed with a worn besom broom, his neighbour, a comely village woman, was brushing away the leaves that had fallen the day before. Her two young daughters, with curly brown hair like their mother's, were playing on the beaten earth of the square, solemnly making piles of bits of wood and pebbles. Feeling Drogtegand's eyes on her, the young woman greeted him curtly and then turned on her heel and went back inside her house.

The villagers, like children who have been scolded by their father, were avoiding Drogtegand this morning. Undaunted, he mechanically plaited his beard in Carolinian style. Then he took up his patriarch's stick and, for the first time in a long while, he got to his feet with difficulty. On days like this, the burden of his years weighed down on him. And yet, he thought, the previous evening's session had actually started quite well. The elders with their long hazel-wood sticks had taken their positions in the middle of the village on an improvised stage which overlooked the assembly. The whole population of the village, both men and women, gathered round them in a compact crowd.

Drogtegand had struck the ground with his staff and the assembled crowd had fallen silent. Edel's awful death had captured their imaginations and sown the seeds of terror among these simple people. They also wanted to know what had happened to Mabille. And Edel, had she really been killed by a werewolf as everyone was saying?

The mystery attached to the young girl's tragic end invited explanations with at least some link to the supernatural, and people spoke in hushed tones of the great goat carcass that was found in the forest not far from Edel's body.

In order to calm the people down, one of the elders had begun to speak, announcing that young Mabille's condition was improving and that she would be back in the village in a few days' time. Her parents, poor peasants who cherished their only daughter, made the sign of the cross with tears in their eyes. Landric the blacksmith, who was a cousin of theirs by marriage, stood next to them, stony faced, holding the small hand of Mabille's younger brother.

But the talk had gradually become more heated and soon questions had been firing from all quarters.

The patriarch stood up and came to the middle of the stage: 'Silence, all of you,' he ordered once more, glowering severely over the assembly.

Roderic stood slightly apart, leaning against a tall oak tree. The young groom had changed beyond all recognition since Edel's death, as if the disappearance of his betrothed had drained him of all substance. He was ashen, and great dark shadows ringed his eyes which burned with a disturbing flame. White streaks had appeared in his black hair, making him look almost like an old man. His father, old Tancard, stood behind him whispering words of comfort which he did not even seem to hear.

A little further on Drogtegand had noticed the noble chevalier accompanied by the strange young monk with the red beard.

Once silence was established again, the patriarch described Edel's disappearance and then the discovery of her remains, trying all the while to avoid giving too many details.

But everything went wrong when some of the villagers returned with the parish priest. The council wanted to question him to find out whether the Dane had been telling the truth about his marriage to the victim.

'Sit down, Father,' said the elder, indicating a bench to the cleric.

'There is no need, I am still on my feet, thank the Lord,' replied the priest, crossing his arms nervously and turning to face the gathered listeners. 'Go ahead.'

'We have called you before the council of elders in order to discover whether you performed a marriage without our being informed.'

The old man flushed slightly, hesitating before he replied. Sensing this, Drogtegand encouraged him gently:

'Speak, Father, no one is being judged here, we know that we have nothing to reproach you for.'

The priest looked up and started to talk very quickly:

'It is true that I married a couple yesterday, Monday, after the revelries, in secret . . . I could not do anything else, Drogtegand.'

A muttering sound welled from the crowd. Roderic, who was standing not far from the old churchman, clenched his fists until his knuckles were white.

'Go on, Father,' said Drogtegand calmly. 'We trust you. If indeed you did bless such a union, going against the rules of our community, you must be able to explain why.'

'I did not have time to let you know and, as I said, I married them without knowing who they were,' stated the priest in a voice that was strangled by emotion. 'And then I admitted it to the Abbot this morning before Nocturn.'

'What did you tell him?' asked Drogtegand.

'I do not know who I married, do you see! The couple forced their way in and, on my doorstep, they pronounced the sacred formula before I could shut them out. The man's hood was lowered, he was tall, though; and the girl's face was hidden by the red bridal veil. I could do nothing other than bless them.'

The old priest's voice was faltering, he looked about anxiously and fell silent.

'I understand,' said the elder with a sigh. 'And you did as you should.'

A weighty silence hovered over the gathering. So it was that Rurik had not lied, he had dared to wed the young girl thereby flouting not only Edel's betrothal but the wishes of both families, and even the entire community of the village who were all related by blood and marriage to a greater or lesser extent.

The mutterings increased until everyone was talking out loud.

Drogtegand raised his staff.

'Silence, all of you! Silence!' he bellowed.

Then he turned to the priest:

'You have nothing to reproach yourself for, Father. You could know no more. If only your blessing could have helped Edel in her terrible fate.'

'Edel was promised to me!' wailed Roderic, coming forward. 'And now she's dead because of that barbarian and, before you all, I call for revenge, Drogtegand.'

'Keep calm, Roderic,' said the old man. 'If Rurik did marry Edel, that does not mean that he killed her.'

'Why then did he flee when they brought the body, if he is as innocent as you say? And why have the men that you sent off on his trail come back empty-handed? Why is he not here before us to defend himself?'

'Yes! Why!' hollered the villagers, raising their fists.

'His flight does not prove his guilt,' Drogtegand retorted calmly. 'It simply proves that he doubts our equity towards him.'

'What do you know about it?' cried Roderic insolently. 'What do we know about this foreigner, anyway?'

'Yes! Yes!' thundered the crowd again.

His face distended with tension, the young groom felt that the crowd was with him. He insisted vehemently: 'The Abbot brought him here, gave him a home and ordered him to lead the fishing. Apart from that, no one here knows anything about him. And because of this accursed foreigner, some of our men died on the day of the whale-hunt and now, not satisfied with that, he steals our women and kills them!'

In saying this Roderic was voicing out loud what everyone wanted to hear.

Drogtegand understood that in these people's simple minds the Dane was already guilty and had been condemned to death. He put down his heavy staff and raised his palms heavenward as a sign of peace.

'Listen to me, all of you, and do not let yourselves be carried away by your anger. We must think. That is the job of the council of elders. That is what you chose us for.'

'It is not time to think any more, it is time to act!' yelled Roderic passionately.

It was the first time for a long while that anyone had stood up to the patriarch. The villagers hesitated for a moment, and then concurred.

'Put him to death! Put him to death!' they chanted. 'Roderic's right, let's catch him, let's kill him.'

'Roderic, your sorrow is robbing you of your reason!' thundered Drogtegand. 'If men died here it was because of the power of the *baloena* and the river, and not because of the Dane. The men of this village behaved like men and died like men. That is all, there is no curse or evil at play.'

The elders nodded their agreement. The patriarch went on: 'As for your intended, Roderic, she could have been killed by a wild beast or by a man, I'll grant you that. But there is nothing to lay the blame on the Dane above anyone else, do you understand!'

'The wild beast is Rurik!' retorted the young groom. 'He's a werewolf. Remember what our ancestors used to say, the Danes used to skewer children alive with their lances, and you think that such a man would hesitate to spill a woman's blood? He's a Dane, he's one of the "race of traitors", he must die!'

Some of the men had raised their pitchforks, some were stamping their feet in fury until the ground shook beneath them.

'Put him to death! Put him to death!'

The women of the village were the most impassioned and

they rallied their menfolk with great cries and chants. After a while, as they could no longer make themselves heard, the elders rose to their feet and filed off the stage behind the patriarch. Drogtegand went over to the young groom and growled: 'That is enough, Roderic, you no longer know what you are saying! There has been too much violence in too short a time and we have lost those that we love. Do you really want to drag these men into more killing? Just like all the others, you chose me to guide you, and I will guide you only towards peace and justice.'

The young man stared at the older man for a moment, then lowered his eyes from his furious gaze.

One of the villagers came over and stood firmly in front of the patriarch. It was Landric, the blacksmith.

'Roderic is right,' he said. 'And you are too, Drogtegand. It is not that anyone doubts what you say, but we want to find the Dane and to avenge Edel. If he is innocent, God will grant him his safety and freedom.'

If men like Landric are going to join in, then there is nothing more for it, thought the old man wearily, seeing the blacksmith's determined expression.

Still he insisted, spelling out his thoughts forcefully.

'You must bring this man back alive and I will give you my word that I will judge him according to our ancient customs, not within the secular judicial system nor that of the abbey.'

'We cannot promise you that, Drogtegand!' one of the young men replied angrily. 'It will not be easy capturing the Dane, so—'

'So you would rather kill him, even if he is innocent!'

'We know that he is guilty,' Roderic cut in abruptly. 'The hunt will be open to everyone from dawn tomorrow.'

'Put him to death! Put the beast to death!' hollered the men as they dispersed with cries and whistles . . .

The die had been cast!

In his heart of hearts, the patriarch hoped that the Dane was out of reach of this baying pack. After all, the three men who had been sent to find him had lost track of him somewhere round Saint-Wandrille. By now he was probably already striding over the roads towards Caudebec, unless he had entered the service of the Lord of Tancarville or another such Norman landlord.

25

Even though it was quite chill that Wednesday morning, on the eve of the great equinox procession, Odon was happy to return to the draughty tranquillity of the cloisters of Jumièges and to the shelter of its arches. He was aware that he had only been at the abbey since Monday and he hoped that this day would offer him more peace and contemplation than the two previous days had.

The mass following the chapter had just come to an end. The young monk had a little over an hour at his disposal until Terce.

He went to the lavatorium which occupied one of the corners of the cloisters and, while he washed his hands, he looked at the sculptures that embellished each of the fine columns. The water gurgled as it flowed away through a narrow stream that ran towards the centre of the cloisters, filling a little stone basin that was used for watering the plants. The leaves of a vine, already tending towards the purples of autumn, climbed right up to the windows of the scriptorium.

In the middle of the courtyard, the freshly turned soil of Joce's grave was still obvious. There, amid the *parterres* of rosemary, thyme and mint, the monks were laid to rest. The priests for their part were interred under the shady arches, nourishing with their bodies the soil that their brothers trod as they meditated.

Odon sighed, mechanically smoothing the hair of his short red beard. He had not lost any time and had already questioned quite a number of monks but, apart from the usual quarrels, had unearthed nothing more than a slight lack of authority on the part of the Abbot. As for the relic, nothing, for now, could explain its disappearance, except perhaps for the crippling financial problems within the abbey. In any event, it was unthinkable for an abbey to sell the sacred remains of its founding saint, nothing like it had ever been done. But you never could tell!

Odon sat down on a bench and picked a little branch of rosemary, pulling off its leaves as he thought. He sent one of the novices to find the Hosteller, and wondered how he would start his conversation with him.

The sound of footsteps made him look up. A solid-looking monk of about fifty years bid him good day and stood waiting with his arms crossed, towering over him.

With his large nose and his fanned out beard, Father Baudri had an unforgettable face. His little grey eyes burned with a sort of irony, and Odon had difficulty analysing his disconcerting attitude.

According to the monks that he had questioned, the Father Hosteller had a reputation as a respectable man.

'You called for me, Brother?' Father Baudri asked abruptly.

'Yes, sit down, Father. Thank you for taking the time to see me. You will not be ignorant of the fact that I am inspecting the abbey on the orders of His Grace the Bishop of Lisieux.'

'Yes, I know that,' replied Father Baudri.

His voice betrayed tension, he seemed to be very wary.

'There is nothing very serious about all this, Father,' soothed Odon, sensing the man's unease.

'Yes, yes,' breathed Baudri. 'How can I be of help to you?'

'Would you mind just answering a few minor questions?' said Odon who carried on tearing out the tiny grey leaves of his rosemary branch one by one.

'I will try,' said the Father Hosteller, surprised by this strange performance and unable to stop himself watching successive leaves falling to the ground.

'Good, tell me first of all, are you from these parts, Father?' asked Odon, essaying a smile.

'I fail to see what that has to do with your enquiry,' the Hosteller retorted rather too quickly.

Odon looked up, dropped the bare branch and went to pick another one before coming and sitting back down and starting the irritating little ritual all over again.

'Oh yes, Father, I am sure that you are right but answer all the same, that way we will have finished all the sooner.'

The Hosteller disclosed unwillingly: 'I am from Duclair. A few leagues from here.'

'What do you think of your Reverend Father the Abbot?' went on Odon who seemed to pay hardly any attention to the other man's replies.

'Oh, he is a godly man, that much is certain.'

'Is that all?'

'He is humble and is exemplary in his charity . . .'

'Yes, yes . . . Are there other monks from the Terre Gémétique like yourself, Father?'

'Um, yes. Brother Anselme, our nurse, he is from Caudebec or Yvetot, I do not quite remember.'

'And your godly Abbot?'

'What of him?'

'Is he from this region too?'

'Um, no, I think not,' replied the Father Hosteller who was disconcerted by these abrupt questions. 'But you should ask the Rector, it is his job to keep the registers, and he would be able to tell you these sort of details better than I.'

'Yes, yes, you are right, I shall think about it,' muttered the little monk, still absorbed with his handiwork. 'I wonder . . .'

Odon stopped, leaving his sentence hanging in the air. Father Baudri clenched his fists. This conversation was really beginning to get on his nerves. He turned to the visitor, who seemed to have forgotten he was even there, and asked curtly: 'What?'

Odon looked up and looked at him thoughtfully.

'What did you wonder, Brother Odon?' said Baudri, raising his voice in spite of himself.

'Oh, nothing very important . . . how do you wake yourself up in the morning for Nocturn?'

'I beg your pardon?' asked Baudri, more and more amazed.

He who had imagined a solemn discussion with a severe-looking monk, found himself in the grip of this strange little man, a youngster to boot, with ridiculous habits and questions he could not make head or tail of!

'How do you wake yourself up for Nocturn?' repeated Odon turning his candid gaze squarely to the Father Hosteller.

'With the bell, of course.'

'Who rings in the first service?'

'It used to be poor Joce, now it is the Sexton, Gachelin.'

'Ah yes, and do you know what he uses as a reference?'

'Sorry?'

'Is it the cockerel *qui excitat fratres ad nocturnas vigilias* – who wakes the brothers for Nocturn?'

'Um, no.'

'It is important, you know, Saint Benoît's law can only be respected if the sequence of services is punctual!' said Odon, carelessly throwing his rosemary branch to the ground. 'Monasteries have been seen descending into chaos because the services were being rung in too late. God likes regularity, my Father, that is how he created the world and the firmament of the skies!'

'Yes, quite so,' replied Baudri, stupefied that Odon should have come out with such a statement.

'So, answer my question,' insisted Odon gently.

'Yes, Brother. Joce used that shrub as his reference,' said the Father Hosteller, indicating a juniper bush in the middle of the monastic garden.

'This shrub here?' said Odon, going over and standing next to it.

'Yes, he would stand there, a bit further to the left.'

'Where the grass is worn away?'

'Yes, just there, and when the evening star was directly above those two windows there, in the middle, you see, he would ring in the service. Of course, his points of reference were not always the same, it depended on the seasons and the weather, but Joce knew the stars better than he knew the Terre Gémétique.'

'Very interesting,' said Odon who was already looking somewhere else. 'And what about your founding saint?'

'What?' said the poor Hosteller who really was having trouble following Odon's train of thought.

'Philibert is an admirable saint, do you not think?' exclaimed Odon, returning to the bench.

'Yes, Brother,' said Baudri, sitting down heavily beside him.

'What do you think of the disappearance of the Abbot's seal and the sacred relic?'

'It is a terrible shame, but I cannot think who would have done such a thing.'

'Oh, I was not asking you that, but now that you come to mention it . . .'

Odon paused for a moment, giving his words time to have their effect on the bigger man.

'Given your very important rôle within the monastery, Father, you might have some idea. You see so many people in the hostel, you hear so much. Might there be someone who attached a very special importance to the sacred relic?'

Baudri stood up abruptly and started pacing backwards and forwards muttering. Odon acted as if nothing had changed, not even looking up to watch him.

'Well then, Father,' he said after a moment, 'what were we saying? Look, as you are up, could you pass me another rosemary branch, please.'

The Father Hosteller hesitated and then tore off a branch sharply and handed it to the monk.

'Thank you so much. Sit down, sit down, Father, you make me giddy going round like that.'

The tall man complied and sat back down next to Brother Odon, and then announced with some difficulty, 'There is actually someone who never forgets to perform his devotion to our sacred founder and who begged the Abbot to accept a gift of a new reliquary encrusted with precious stones and engraved with his initials . . .'

'Indeed?' said the little monk, sounding almost bored.

'It is the old Lord of Clères. He will be devastated when he learns that the relic has disappeared, he never failed to offer countless alms and devotions to it. But he is so ill at the moment—'

'So it was the Sexton who rang the bells yesterday morning, for the first time?' said Odon, interrupting Father Baudri. 'I'm sorry, what did you say?'

'Oh, nothing. I was thinking,' the Father Hosteller replied dryly. 'Did you hear what I said about the Lord of Clères?'

'Oh, yes, yes, of course,' replied Odon distractedly. 'But what did you say about the bells?'

The Father Hosteller shrugged his shoulders and lowered his voice: 'It was not yesterday morning, it was the day before yesterday, on Monday morning that Brother Gachelin rang in Nocturn.'

'Are you sure, the very day I arrived?'

'Why yes. We even woke a little late. No one knows the stars as well as Joce, from now on we will have to do as they do at Saint-Wandrille or at Bec Helloüin, use hourglasses or candles.'

'You say that it was too late?'

'Yes, my brother.'

'You are invaluable to me, Father. I am told the Conihout wine is so acidic that you have to dilute it more than is usual?'

The churchman opened his eyes wide with amazement, but Odon pursued his train of thought sententiously.

'Fortuitously Saint Benoît's law only accords us one half measure a day. I have known monks in the good town of Dijon put away three or four litres of mixed wine a day, but it was probably better than yours here, because they enjoyed it!'

Baudri stayed silent.

'Apparently the locals round here even have a saying: "He who drinks of the Conihout wine, will do evil ere the clock strikes nine."'

'Brother Odon, the Conihout wine is what it is but, if you want to talk to someone about it, our Cellarer, Onfroi, would be more familiar with the subject than myself. Have you already seen him?

'Do not hold it against me, but I must return to my duties,' said the Hosteller rising to his feet, poorly disguising his icy anger with a smile.

'Oh, Father, forgive me. Time flies so quickly. I am like the quadrants lit up by the sun, *Non numero horas nisi serenas*, I only see the hours of daylight. Go in peace, Father, may God keep watch over you, and would you kindly have the Sexton, Brother Gachelin, sent to me.'

'Very well, Brother, I will take care of it,' replied Father Baudri turning on his heel and forgetting to return Odon's farewell.

The sound of the robust hosteller's footsteps faded away and a cunning smile crept over the little monk's face.

When Brother Gachelin arrived in the cloisters he did not immediately see the little monk.

Kneeling under the arches of the cloisters, Odon was absorbed in the contemplation of a basement window protected by sturdy bars.

'Brother, you sent for me,' said an impatient voice ringing out high and clear.

Odon stood up again and shook his habit which was covered in dust, before looking at the monk standing before him.

'Brother Gachelin, I presume. Tell me, where does this window lead?'

'It is one of the windows into the abbey's wine cellars.'

'I did not know that the Jumièges wines were so precious that they needed bars to protect them!'

'You are right, but it is also said that it was once a prison for any men of God who violated their vows. The old monks tell stories of prisoners chained to the walls. Close to them, but just out of reach, was a lighted candle, a piece of bread and a bowl of water. The doors would be closed and then they would wait for the cries to die down and for the rats to clear up the remains . . .'

'*Vade in pace*, go in peace . . . now, there is a pretty story, would you not say. I prefer the wine cellar version, even though the dilute wine that we drink in the frater is not really to my taste.'

'Certainly, wine does not come much worse than that,' agreed the Sexton. 'Luckily the Abbot sometimes has barrels of wine brought in from Saint-Germain-des-Prés or from Anjou.'

While the monk was speaking, Odon took note of his powerful frame and square shoulders. The Sexton was a good-looking man, and young too. He was outspoken and wore his humble habit as others might wear a handsome leather tunic.

'I have been told, Father,' said Odon in a gentle voice, 'that you were given to the monastery as an oblation?'

A glimmer passed over the monk's green eyes. He winced.

'And you were told the truth. I was given to Jumièges at the age of nine . . .'

'I have been told,' continued Odon in the same calm tone, 'that you were the son of a Lord but only the second son, and that your father, wanting to favour his first-born, chose this way of providing for you: putting you under God's protection and that of the sacred founder of Jumièges.'

The Sexton's regular features were distorted for a moment by a grimace, he crossed his arms and looked the monk squarely in the eye, replying heatedly, 'And you were told the truth! Which fetid serpent has spilt this venom?'

Despite the insolent tone of his voice, Odon did not reply, content to wait for a further reaction from the Sexton.

'And what can I, Gachelin, a penniless oblation, do for you, Brother, since you already know so much about me?'

Odon sighed. There was a measure of compassion in his eye when he announced: 'I think, Brother, that you are not at peace with yourself and that you do not wear this habit easily. In fact, I think that your choice *non erat tutat viae incendendi per viam salutis* is not the best route along the pathway of your happiness.'

Gachelin paled and then moved closer to the monk and glowered.

'How do you dare to say such a thing?'

'Better that I should say it,' retorted Odon calmly, 'than write what I know or talk about it to your Abbot, who seems to be a saintly man, although he is too indulgent for my tastes.'

'Explain yourself!' said Gachelin in a voice strangled by anger.

The furious monk's emotions seemed to slip off Odon like water off a duck's back. He turned his dark eyes to the Sexton and replied quietly: 'But no, Brother, I do not have to explain myself. Let us stop all this pretence here and now; I will offer you a deal.'

'By what right? You have absolutely no power over me,' thundered the Sexton.

'Oh but I do, Brother,' said Odon. 'It is not a question of power. Whether you are the son of a Lord or, like myself, the son of a labourer, do not forget that here we are all equals in the face of divine punishment.'

Gachelin clenched his fists but said nothing.

'As for my rôle,' the little monk continued, 'it is to write a report: *Puram veritatem simplicibus verbis*, nothing but the truth, pure and simple. And it shall be so, believe me. So, listen, either you confess of all your sins, all of them, do you understand! Or . . .'

'Or?' asked Gachelin seeming suddenly worried.

'Or I will see to it that you suffer a worse fate than that reserved for the monks of yesteryear!'

The Sexton turned to the little monk with an anxious expression. Odon's calm determination seemed to have got the better of Gachelin's choler. After a brief hesitation, he whispered: 'Give me time to think, Brother, give me a little time.'

'I will give you until tomorrow, same time, same place,' said Odon severely. 'May God protect you from yourself and may He bring you counsel.'

26

Since fleeing from the village, Rurik had actually scarcely travelled any distance. He had been going round in circles, not knowing what to do any more. Whereas on the morning itself he had been thinking only of taking revenge on Edel, her brutal death left him bereft of everything, of his loathing and of his passion for her.

He had toyed with the three men that Drogtegand had sent to track him down, leading them all the way to Saint-Wandrille and then, having set them on that course, he turned back towards Jumièges, still at a run.

He certainly had thought of reaching Caudebec, but he was obsessed by the memory of the shroud. He wanted to see the body and to know how she had died. Had he struck her too hard? She was so fragile and delicate. But, no, he remembered the way she looked as he went out, she looked as if she were in pain, but she was very much alive . . .

Exhausted, famished, his muscles cramped by prolonged effort, he had eventually taken refuge at the abandoned quarries of Trou de Fer. He knew that there, at least, no one would come looking for him. The people of the peninsula were superstitious. So many men had died in this sinister place that they believed demons inhabited the rocks and blew out the torches of those who ventured too far, losing them for ever in the infernal underground maze.

Having already spent a night here when he was out hunting, Rurik knew somewhere that he could take shelter and hide.

He drank a little of the filthy opaque water that oozed up through the chalky rocks and ate a few sour blackberries before slipping into a narrow crevasse and sitting with his back to the wall and his axe between his thighs. He put his head on his arms and sank into a deep sleep.

When he woke in the morning, the sun was already high and

he could hear the sound of furious barking reverberating in the distance. Seeing their men coming back empty-handed, the villagers must have set off after me with their dogs, thought the Dane.

He would have to move quickly if he was to throw the animals off his scent. He grabbed his axe and slithered out of the crack, quickly glancing round before disappearing into the thickets.

The night gives good counsel, and Rurik now knew what he must do. He must ask for God's protection and seek asylum in the abbey. The Abbot Eustache would be able to protect him, or at least Rurik hoped he would, from the unswerving hatred of the locals.

The Dane fled, leaping over bushes, using paths known to him alone, or so he believed, when he suddenly came across a group of about ten men armed with pitchforks and sticks.

The peasants froze for a moment, watching their adversary warily, before starting to yell and scream as if to build up their courage.

'At him! At him! Death to the Dane! Death to the beast!'

And they charged, pitchforks lowered.

The young man looked round hastily. The path was narrow here, edged by great boulders along the cliffs. To the right he could get back to the banks of the Seine and hide in the marshes, to the left, he could cross the woods that he knew better than his adversaries and get to the abbey.

He let out a hoarse war cry and, swinging his axe, lunged at the band of men who scattered back on impact, the handles of their pitchforks snapped by the Dane's iron blade. Making the most of this moment of confusion, Rurik leapt into the bushes and ran off to the nearby forest where he disappeared.

But that did not take into account the dogs.

Four villagers led by Landric the blacksmith, had heard their companions' railing and subsequent shouts of anger. They started to run and caught up with the others on the fringes of the wood. Landric and his men came to a stop, breathing heavily, the Dane was already too far away. Seeing his tall figure melting into the cover of the trees, the blacksmith gave a yell and set his mastiffs after him.

'Seek; seek him out! Kill him!'

With their noses to the wind, the animals leapt forward. They had locked onto their prey.

Rurik accelerated, his head leaning forward, his elbows tucked into his powerful torso. Great drops of acrid-smelling sweat dripped from his entire body, drawing on the pack that pursued him.

He could now hear the dogs' rasping breath behind him and the sound of twigs snapping in their path. He lengthened his stride again, but knew that he would not be able to maintain such a speed for long. His legs were stiffening with the effort. He would have to face them.

He slowed, turned round, balanced squarely on his feet and with his axe raised, waited for the beasts to charge.

The two mastiffs sprang out of the bushes growling, with their lips drawn back and their tongues hanging out. They were on him in an instant. The most terrible mêlée followed. The young man managed to duck the first dog by throwing himself to the ground, and he cut off its leg with one swipe of the axe. The creature collapsed, howling, with blood pulsing from the stump.

The second dog, making the most of the diversion, had come round the young man and leapt onto his back, piercing his leather hunting cape with its teeth. The young Dane rolled on the ground to throw it off, but the animal would not release its grip. It had been trained and could stay like this for a long time with its sharp teeth sunk firmly into the man's flesh.

With a desperate leap, Rurik got back to his feet and, with the dog still on his back, he threw himself against a tree, crushing the animal's head against the trunk. The dog was knocked out and it slumped to the ground. Rurik killed it with one blow of his axe.

The Dane bent over and tried to catch his breath. He was in pain, the animal had dug deeply into his flesh, and a long stream of blood now ran down his back.

He had eliminated the dogs but knew that their masters would not be far behind, he would have to run on, no time to rest. He wiped his axe blade on his hose and set off again, burying himself deeper in the forest.

Just a few moments later, the villagers jostled into the clearing. Landric swore when he saw the two dogs on the ground. With a swift stroke of his knife he finished off the one that was still alive and, without wasting any more time, started looking over the humid grass for traces of the Dane's footsteps.

'He went that way!' he roared pointing out a footprint. 'And he's wounded . . . Look, look, there is blood on the leaves, the mastiffs did get him. The beast has been touched, we shall catch him. He cannot keep up this pace for long. You and you, go back to the village to get reinforcements and tell them that the monster is injured. You six block off the road to Yainville in case he tries to head off that way.'

And, without waiting, Landric ran off into the woods followed by five strong men. The trail was very visible with clear footprints and drops of blood here and there along the path as well as crushed vegetation where the young foreigner had passed. Not for one second did the villagers suspect the trap that he was setting for them.

They had rather too quickly forgotten that the Dane was the best hunter in the region and that, despite his wounds, the rôle of prey would be hardly to his taste. Having left a few obvious footprints for their benefit, Rurik had then stuffed his tunic with moss to staunch the flow of blood from the wound, and with the help of a leafy branch he had erased his footsteps as he went, before setting off at a run again and describing a large circle that brought him back just behind his pursuers.

A gap had opened up between the villagers. Landric was a swift runner and he had taken the lead, followed by three of his companions. Far behind, two other men were already exhausted by this flat out pursuit and had themselves fallen back. One cry – muffled by the thick foliage – and they lay on the ground, struck down.

The Dane swiftly cut up their leather hunting cloaks with the blade of his weapon. He bound and gagged them with the wide strips of leather and then set off again. Another straggler suffered the same fate a little further on, then another.

The vegetation was becoming more and more dense. The branches whipped the blacksmith's face. Quite out of breath, Landric came to an abrupt halt, realising that there was no longer a trail in front of him. The footprints had mysteriously disappeared and, without his dogs, he felt lost.

A wall of virgin, untouched vegetation rose up before him and in one of the trees over his head a little red squirrel seemed to be chattering mockingly at him. The blacksmith turned to tell his comrades that he had lost the trail but there was no one behind him any more. He listened carefully, he could hear no footsteps. He called out in a voice that grated with anxiety. In vain. He was alone. Only the distorted echo of his own words answered him, mingled with the sounds of the wind in the great leaves. He wondered anxiously where his companions had disappeared to.

For the first time, Landric took fright. Not because of Rurik, but because of the dark forest that surrounded him, this wood that he had never entered and in which he felt like a stranger. Everything here was moist and humid, like a woman's belly after her passion was spent.

Long strands of grey-green moss covered the knotty trunks. Drops of dew fell from one leaf to another before splattering onto the black humus. A powerful smell of decomposition bore down on him.

He crossed himself briskly. He did not belong here. He had unwittingly ventured into the depths of the forest, which did not like to be disturbed, violated, by men.

A muffled sound from a nearby thicket of bushes made him jump.

Hating himself for his own cowardice, Landric pulled himself together and with a resolute face and a hard-set jaw he stood at the ready with his lance in his hand, and yelled furiously: 'Come closer, damn you, you cursed foreigner! I am not afeared of you, come on, come and fight me like a man! I'm waiting!'

There was no reply.

The Dane was far away. He had been running again for a while now, having decided to use the last of his strength to reach the abbey, hoping that he would be able to slip inside under cover of darkness.

27

Galeran and Brother Odon had met up by the abbey's vivarium, as they had agreed the previous evening. The two men walked as they spoke, following the long line of beeches that bordered the pools of fish. From time to time, a trout would leap to catch an insect.

'What do you think about it then?' Odon asked the chevalier when he had related his conversations with Father Baudri and the Sexton.

'I think, Brother,' replied Galeran gravely, 'that if one of those two men is the assassin, you took a considerable risk in pressing him like that with your questions.'

'I do not think he is capable of murder, and yet . . .' Odon murmured, so quietly that the chevalier could hardly hear him.

'Who do you mean?'

'The Sexton. Listen, this is what the Rector told me. As I told you, Gachelin came here as an oblation, he was given to the monastery of Jumièges by his father when he was just nine years old. He is no more or less than the younger son of Lord de Clères.'

'De Clères . . .' Galeran repeated. 'De Clères, we have heard that name before. Oh yes, I remember, it was the name of the young nobleman that we met on this very spot, the day we arrived.'

'Quite so. Whatever one might be led to believe, our little Sexton is related to the most powerful family in the region after the Tancarvilles, and his high birth has not stopped him becoming one of God's paupers . . .'

'Pauper? I would not go that far,' retorted the chevalier with a smile. 'Did your rector mention the funeral rights from which Gachelin benefits as the Sexton of Jumièges?'

'Yes, I heard about that, an ancient right which goes right back to the foundation of the abbey. And so . . . ?'

'And so, if I am to believe the Porter's son whose tongue can fairly wag, the Sexton is actually quite well off, and his wealth comes straight from the larceny he commits helping himself to the property of the dead. Tancard and Drogtegand both told me that he had a house on the Yainville road.'

'The Yainville road, is that not the road we took yesterday, to reach the sanatorium?'

'Why yes. The Sexton is hardly run-of-the-mill, I think you will agree. He has his own house, near the pest-house. He is well known, nay notorious – even in the village, I checked – for his amorous adventures. At the feast, he had eyes only for Edel and . . .'

'And what?' asked Odon impatiently.

'Poor Joce was under his orders!'

'Indeed,' murmured Odon. 'I had forgotten him, poor soul!'

'In a word, this Gachelin seems to me to have a good many sins to confess, my brother, and will have some difficulty avoiding the *peona gravissima*, the ultimate punishment,' declared the chevalier, looking the monk directly in the eye.

'It is still strange, though,' said Odon dreamily, 'everyone here seems to know about this character's behaviour and yet he has been doing as he pleases for many years, flouting all the rules while no one actually does aught to stop him.'

'The world will always prefer Barabbas!' declared the chevalier with a smile. 'People willingly accuse a man with means, but they will always find excuses for the crook!'

'Well, never mind. Do you know what?' replied Odon in his soft voice.

'Oh, I think I can guess!'

'Let us say, then, that I find this particular Barabbas too much of a slave to the flesh to be the man we are looking for . . . but perhaps I am mistaken,' Odon added wisely.

'But he was the one who rang in Nocturn, you told me.'

'Yes, and I think, as you do, that poor Joce was already dead then,' said the little man, running his hand through his beard '. . . but, my Lord Galeran, as for Nocturn you are right and you are wrong!'

'Pray go on, Odon.'

'Well, you see, if Nocturn had been rung on time, I would

have said that you were right and that it was the assassin who pulled the bell-rope. Only, Father Baudri told me that on that particular morning Nocturn was rung late, I checked, it is true, and there—'

'There you think that I am wrong,' said the chevalier with a laugh, 'and you are probably right, Brother. My reasoning does not stand up. Gachelin, in his capacity as Sexton, should know his assistant's references to astronomical movements and other methods, he should have rung it on time unless he was held up elsewhere. I think we need to look further. But I must confess, my dear Odon, that it is a pleasure discussing this with someone with a mind as sharp as yours.'

'The feeling is mutual, my Lord,' said the monk with his mocking little smile. 'What are you going to do now?'

'I was thinking of going to see Lord de Clères, whose son opportunely disappeared the very night that Edel was killed and the seal seems to have vanished.'

'Do you think . . .'

'I think only one thing, Odon, and that is that the family is linked, however tenuously, to the disappearance of the sacred reliquary.'

'It is true, that Father Baudri admitted to me that Lord de Clères was truly passionate about the relic of Saint Philibert. It was even he who donated the precious reliquary in which it was kept,' added Odon. 'But Galeran, they say the old man is at death's door. Your visit is hardly likely to be much appreciated.'

'It matters not. Anyway, it is the only lead that we have at the moment, and the procession is to take place tomorrow morning. We will have to act quickly if we want the abbey to repossess its valuables in time. And, what is more, relics are highly sought after in these hard times. You know as well as I do that there are monasteries prepared to pay very high prices in order to acquire them, especially if they are connected with a saint as famous as Philibert.'

Odon smoothed his short beard.

'Quite so, my Lord. As for me, I will carry on with my enquiries.'

'While we are on the subject, Odon, something happened last night that I did not fully understand. I was not sleeping very well, and I was woken by screaming coming from the infirmary. According to the Hosteller there was someone there who was ill, as well as the Friar Nurse, the Sexton and the Reverend Abbot himself. They would not let me in. Perhaps you could find out what was going on.'

'I heard nothing, but I will find out, my Lord. Ah, by the way,' murmured the monk after a moment, 'this so-called green wolf, this Jendeus that you asked me to find, he was definitely put up in the hostelry, his arrival was entered in the register held by the Rector, only . . .'

'Only?'

'Only, he is no longer there. And, according to the register, he never left . . .' said Odon, his little smile playing on the edges of his lips.

The chevalier pouted and shrugged his shoulders. Odon did exasperate him sometimes!

Eventually, the two men parted having arranged to meet in the same place the next day.

Galeran made his way calmly to the stables to get his charger, and Odon went back to continue his enquiries in the abbey.

28

Since he did not know the way to Lord de Clères' property, the chevalier asked for directions from Roderic.

At a time when all the villagers, or almost all of them, had gone to track down the Dane, the young groom had not joined the hunt after all but had returned to the abbey to continue with his duties in the stables, tending to the horses.

Galeran had found him bedding down the stalls. He was still terribly pale and worked on in silence. The chevalier watched him for a moment before coughing to indicate his presence.

'It is you, my Lord,' murmured Roderic without even looking round.

The young man's voice was so weak that the chevalier had to come closer to hear him.

'It is I, Roderic. I have come for my charger,' he said gently.

'He has been groomed and fed. I will go and get your tack, my Lord.'

'Leave it, Roderic, I will manage very well on my own. Just tell me how I can get to the de Clères' family property.'

Roderic answered in a flat, monotonous voice, staring absently at his pitchfork.

'You have to go to Duclair, and then to Barentin, then you take the track along by the river, the Clérette. It will take you straight to them.'

'Thank you kindly, Roderic, may God protect you,' said Galeran as he moved off to get his tack.

Once the chevalier had left, Roderic looked up. He ran a trembling hand through his white-streaked hair and cried out: 'God! God . . . God has forgotten me, my Lord, damn Him! Damn Him!'

The pitchfork hurtled through the air and quivered as it pierced the ground.

Once he had left the abbey, Galeran gave Quolibet a good kick and the horse gratefully lengthened his stride before breaking into an all out gallop. Some cottars on the track hastily stood aside: it was as well not to stand in the way of a galloping war-horse.

Riding along parallel to the Seine, the chevalier soon reached the little village of Duclair.

As in Jumièges, wide rafts travelled back and forth between the banks, transporting goods and passengers. A little white stone church stood in the centre of the shady little square. The elderly sat chatting on their doorsteps. Galeran patted Quolibet's neck and then jumped to the ground, taking hold of the bridle to lead the gelding to a water trough. He greeted the villagers courteously, speaking to them for quite a while before setting off again towards Barentin which he cut across without stopping.

After following the sinuous course of the Clérette, the chevalier saw at last the imposing fortress that had been Gachelin's family home. The chevalier kicked his horse on and cut through mesne and the outbuildings – practically a town in their own right comprising long-houses, stables and barns – which stood between him and the main entrance to the manor. The estates were well kept and the villeins, bent over their work, did not even look up as he passed.

The de Clères château was surrounded by a rampart of earth and a sturdy wall, and was built of hewn stone. It was a great square building flanked by four hefty towers, one at each corner.

The chevalier announced himself at the watch and, having said that he came on the Abbot's recommendation, he was allowed in straight away. He passed under the fortified porch, and came into a large courtyard which boasted a little chapel and a brick dovecote.

Once he had tied Quolibet to a ring, Galeran noticed a servant who had come to greet him. He was the castle's bailiff, a bulky man whose grey complexion and sad expression betrayed his manifold worries. Beckoning the chevalier to follow him, he went through a vaulted entrance and into a vast communal hall where a great fire roared, despite the mild weather.

'Sit down, my Lord, I beg you,' he said indicating a large settle next to the hearth.

'There is no need, thank you, I will remain standing.'

'Forgive my greeting, my Lord, but my master, in his present state, cannot receive you. He is in a very bad way. What can I do for you?'

'I have been sent by the Abbot Eustache. I come to offer my best wishes to your master, Lord de Clères,' the chevalier murmured, as if confidentially, 'and to ask after his health.'

'The Abbot Eustache at Jumièges, but . . .'

'But?'

'Um, I sincerely hope he has not changed his mind.'

'About what, my friend?'

'I know not whether I should . . .'

'Speak, my friend!' ordered the chevalier.

The bailiff hesitated, but the young chevalier's frank face seemed determined.

'About the priest, my Lord.'

The conversation was going in an unexpected direction.

'Well, to tell you the truth, the Abbot would like to discuss the matter further with your master and that is why I have come,' replied the chevalier with aplomb.

The man groaned and allowed himself to fall with all his bulk onto a stool: 'It is impossible, it is impossible . . .'

'Calm down, my good man, and explain yourself,' said Galeran authoritatively.

The bailiff gulped and sat up.

'My Lord chevalier, please forgive me. But my Lord Rainolf is out hunting and I do not know whether I should . . .'

'Speak!' ordered Galeran again.

'My master paid a high price to keep this sacred relic by his side, and my Lord Rainolf told us that the Abbot gave him permission, he made an exception, out of respect for my master's devotion to Saint Philibert. But to take it back now would be a fatal blow, I fear!'

'Who said anything about taking the relic away?' said an imperious voice behind the chevalier. 'And who are you? I know you not, my Lord.'

Galeran turned round and immediately recognised the haughty character that he had seen parading at the hostelry in Jumièges. Rainolf de Clères was tall and well turned out but he was afflicted with a fleshy, blotchy face. He was eyeing the chevalier arrogantly, waiting for a reply to his question.

A subtle smile drew up the corners of Galeran's fine mouth: 'Galeran de Lesneven, Breton knight,' he said, 'but I know you, my Lord. You are Rainolf de Clères, elder brother of Gachelin, the Sexton of Jumièges, unless I am mistaken.'

The man's face drained of its colour and he retorted insolently: 'So what? That does not explain why you are here within these walls.'

'I was sent by the Abbot Eustache, my Lord.'

'The Reverend Father sent you! But what on earth does he want from me?'

'From you, nothing for the moment, my Lord. He would simply like to take back Saint Philibert's relic.'

'But you must be mad! What are you saying? As if we had a relic here!' retorted the other haughtily.

'Your bailiff was just talking to me about the one by your father's bedside – in his chamber, I believe. For your part, you have a very short memory because you seemed to know about it when you first came into this room.'

The poor bailiff, who was listening to the conversation, flinched under Rainolf's furious stare.

'Out, you good-for-nothing,' he growled. 'I'll deal with you later, and you will suffer for this!'

Without a word, the bailiff lumbered out as fast as he could.

'And now?' said Galeran quietly.

'I am sure we can come to some sort of arrangement,' Rainolf ventured in an unctuous voice.

'Quite so, my Lord, in fact there are two different possible arrangements and I am beginning to think I prefer the first. If you carry on with this little charade, I will give you a taste of my sword and I will leave with the relic whether you like it or not – that is the first option. Or . . .'

'Or?' Rainolf asked anxiously.

'Or, you will go and get the aforementioned relic instantly, without making any more trouble, and I will leave you to the pleasure of explaining the situation to your unfortunate father.'

'You are mistaken, Chevalier, it was Gachelin who arranged all of this,' whined the other.

'I am quite sure your brother helped you in this, in some way. But, as it happens, you are the elder brother and you carry far more of the responsibility for all this than he does.'

'It was for my father, he is dying, I wanted to find some way of comforting him,' pleaded Rainolf, casting his eyes to the heavens.

'You bring tears to my eyes, Rainolf,' snapped the chevalier. 'That is enough, you will have to live with your macabre jokes, your plot has failed. The Abbot would never have loaned you the relic, especially on the eve of the equinox procession. And what about the money that you must have extorted from your father to fund this so-called loan, who was that for? For the poor and destitute, was it, or have you kept it in your own coffers?'

'How did you know? I—'

'Furthermore,' interrupted the chevalier, 'I am prepared to wager that if your father dies, you have already found a buyer, there is no shortage of traders for that sort of thing!'

'But I—' protested Rainolf.

'Stop this performance, which fails to fool anyone, or by God I will not sully my sword on you but I shall beat you with my bare hands like the ruffian that you are.'

The other man paled but did not falter.

'I could call my men . . .'

'You could,' replied Galeran.

After a moment's hesitation, Rainolf finally lowered his head and made his way slowly to the door.

'I will fetch the relic, my Lord,' he said with a strained smile.

When he returned, de Clères was carrying the Saint Philibert reliquary.

'Now, Rainolf, go back to your father's side,' Galeran ordered, 'and comfort him with these words; the Abbot will come to see him soon with the sacred relic. As for you, the Reverend Eustache will receive you alone, tomorrow after Saint Philibert's procession. Be punctual. Until then, I hold you responsible for your father's life. If anything should happen to him, I will make you pay for it, you can be sure of that.'

The chevalier spoke with a menacing edge in his voice. Rainolf nodded and swallowed hard. He stood rooted to the spot before Galeran, awkwardly holding the reliquary at arm's length.

Sickened, the chevalier snatched the precious container from him and strode out of the room.

In the end, the enigma of the reliquary had been easy to solve, thought Galeran as he galloped back to Jumièges. That very evening, he would go to see the Father Abbot and would discreetly return the relic that meant so much to the abbey. As for the other problems within the community, it would be up to cunning little Odon to sort them out, and Galeran had no doubt that he would.

While his horse carried him speedily back, Galeran thought about something altogether different. What continued to disturb him was Edel's mysterious death. Edel had been silenced for ever and there were only two people who knew something of her last hours: her assassin . . . and Mabille. He proposed to deal with this mystery at first light the next day.

PART FOUR

May the fire that consumes me be such
That it could no more be quenched by a flood
Than a silken thread could support a tower of
  mud

Guilhem de Cabestanh, XIIth century

29

Lady Frédesande had a handsome dower and lived in a hermitage not far from the pest-house. She was an energetic woman of about forty who had devoted herself to the poorest of the poor ever since she was widowed. The monks would often ask for her help, and she had willingly agreed to look after Mabille.

Early on the morning of 21st September, far from the bustle of Jumièges, she went into Mabille's little cell carrying a large basin full of water.

The young girl was still huddled on her mattress with her back to the wall, her face unwashed and her hair unkempt. She did, however, seem to be calmer. A great silence reigned in the small chamber. Without a word, the widow put the basin down on the ground and went out.

She came back almost immediately carrying over her arm a bundle of underclothes and garments which she arranged on the bed in front of Mabille in silence.

There was a kirtle of blue cloth, petticoats, a cambric shift, a Rouen shawl, a little white linen bonnet, stockings and a pair of suede shoes with silver buckles.

The young girl's eyes alighted on the shoes, and then on Lady Frédesande's welcoming face. She twisted her face as if to push back her tears, and a little colour returned to her cheeks. She put out her hand and, snatching up one of the shoes, she examined it as if it were a treasure. Finally, she looked up and asked hesitantly: 'Who is it for?'

'It is for you, gentle Mabille, you cannot stay dirty as you are, with your torn dress . . .'

'Are the shoes for me?' insisted the young girl.

'Of course, and the other things too.'

'I have never worn such lovely things . . .'

'Well, you shall wear them all the same! But first, you need to eat something. Then you will get up and come and have a wash,' said the widow firmly.

Mabille, enthralled, meekly downed a large bowl of gruel, then Lady Frédesande took her by the hand and helped her to her feet. She could hardly stand up, and the kindly woman had to help her over to the basin of water. A turn of the hourglass later Mabille was unrecognisable, her waist becomingly accentuated in the new blue kirtle, her slender feet prettily shod, and her hair finely plaited. The little white bonnet framed her young face and complemented her sweet, yet serious expression.

At that moment the chevalier came in. He looked from the widow to Mabille, barely recognising her.

'Why, without a word of a lie, Lady Frédesande, you have performed a miracle!'

The lady made a little curtsey and said mockingly: 'This miracle was not my doing, my Lord, it was Mistress Mabille who helped the most.'

Galeran turned to the young girl.

'How are you feeling this morning, fair damsel?'

The girl gave a bemused smile and, lifting up her skirts, stretched out her childlike foot.

'I have shoes,' she said earnestly.

Galeran and Lady Frédesande burst out laughing. After a moment's stunned silence, Mabille joined them. Her head was swimming slightly, as if she had drunk too much sparkling wine, and she let herself fall back onto the bed laughing.

Lady Frédesande withdrew discreetly, and the chevalier sat down next to the young girl. After a moment he said softly: 'Gentle Mabille, would it displease you to speak of Edel now?'

The girl listened to him, with her chin in her hands, staring blankly ahead.

'No,' she said with a deep sigh. 'I have been ill for a long time have I not?'

'Yes, but that is quite normal. You did not want to believe that your friend was dead, and you shut out the things you had seen; Providence took pity on you and allowed you to forget.'

'Did I speak? Did I talk nonsense?'

'No, you just moaned between your teeth, and it meant nothing.'

The girl seemed relieved.

'But now, Mabille,' said the chevalier, 'you can help me. Whoever mistreated your friend must have the punishment he deserves, and must not be allowed to harm anyone else. Do you not agree?'

Mabille merely sighed, nodding her head vaguely.

'Now then, Edel was your best friend,' said the chevalier. 'She must have confided in you. She must have told you things.'

The girl pulled a funny face: 'Oh yes, she often told me things. But, do you see, my Lord, I do not want to talk about it because it made me ashamed for her. And, anyway, she has sworn me to secrecy on the cross, and I cannot go back on my word . . . No, my Lord I cannot betray her!'

So that was how things stood, Mabille might have manifold things to tell him but Galeran sensed that she would remain silent and stand by her promise. He, therefore, affected resignation.

'I am aggrieved to hear it, but I understand you. So you do not wish to be of help to me?'

'I cannot be sure, I am afraid, you see . . . What happened to Edel, it was so terrible . . . how did Rurik end up doing something like that, has he not been caught?'

'You think that it was the Dane who did that to your friend?'

'Who else? or otherwise it was a werewolf,' she said, her eyes popping out of her head.

'All right, listen. The Dane has evaded capture thus far but he will be caught sooner or later. Never fear, he will have to explain himself. Now, tell me, do you feel strong enough to go home to your village? If you agree to it, I will take you home to your sorrowing family straight away.'

Mabille smiled slightly, 'On your horse?'

'On my horse,' Galeran replied seriously.

'Well then, I would like to,' said the young girl, with a sigh of wonderment.

A little later she was saying her farewells to the charitable widow and the Friar Nurse, who watched her with wide eyes and deeply flushed cheeks.

Galeran leapt onto Quolibet and lifted the feather-light girl in front of him.

'How strange,' he thought to himself as he kicked his horse into a canter, 'on the day of the revelries Mabille was but a child still, and suddenly she is transformed, a slip of a woman who already senses her comeliness!'

30

Prime had ended and the officiators, followed by the monks, were filing one by one into the chapter house.

In this vast room above the hall of relics, they held the *conventus* – the priests' assembly – every morning, making important decisions concerning the smooth running of the abbey.

High torches illuminated the room and two rows of wooden benches were arranged facing each other. At the end of the alley formed by the benches stood the Reverend Abbot's imposing sedilia and two lecterns, one for the Holy Bible and the other for the laws of Saint Benoît.

As on every other morning, before the assembly took place, a monk had cleaned the floor and the woodwork and a pleasant smell of wax hung in the air. The windows were opened onto the monastic gardens and let in the plaintive singing of the birds woken by the glow of dawn. There was a table set up next to the central bay and covered with a white linen cloth. A bunch of flowering hyssop had been put there by the Chaplain.

Still silent, the monks made their way to their usual places, the officiators took their seats at the ends of the rows, to the right and the left of the Abbot's sedilia. The only sounds were the rasping of their sandals on the paving slabs and the slight rustling of their habits.

The Prior, who had gone to stand next to the Abbot's sedilia, clapped his hands together and everyone froze.

The Father Abbot made his entrance. He walked slowly through the gathered monks, briefly inclining his head from time to time, before reaching his sedilia and standing in front of it.

In honour of the forthcoming procession, he was already wearing a long gold-edged chasuble in which he did not look at ease, and he raised the imposing sleeves awkwardly. Brother Odon followed him, solemnly holding at arm's length a large object draped in fabric.

The Abbot invited the young visitor to put the object down on the table in front of the window and, contrary to custom, to come and sit down beside him. The monks made way and moved up for Odon grudgingly. This was going to be a very unusual assembly.

'Sit down, my brothers, and let us meditate today on a text from our sacred law,' said Father Abbot.

After a deep, respectful silence, he opened the compendium of laws created in the 6th century by Saint Benoît, the founder of the Benedictine order, and declared solemnly, 'I have chosen for you this morning a passage from our law which concerns our brothers who are given to us as oblations. Hear, my brothers, what Saint Benoît orders us to do:

"If it should happen that a nobleman offers his son to God in the monastery, his parents will promise on oath that never by their doing, nor in any way, will they give him an opportunity to own anything. Thus any means of leaving will be blocked to that child, any thought that might seduce him and lose him – may God preserve him – as experience has instructed us."'

A heavy silence followed his words.

'Let us pray, my brothers,' said the Abbot kneeling down.

Only Gachelin remained standing, hesitating, his face twisted with tension. He was the only oblation in the community and could not help but feel targeted by Abbot Eustache's words. The Prior threw him a stern look and indicated that he should get down on his knees like his brothers.

As he complied, with an angry jerk, Gachelin thought to himself that Odon had lost no time getting to work. Even before Nocturn he had let the little monk know that he refused to confess and would, therefore, not meet him as they had arranged the day before. He had not had to wait long for the next development.

There was no doubt whatsoever that the little monk must have discussed the matter with the Abbot and revealed to him what he knew about the Sexton's actions, therefore forcing the Abbot to exert his authority.

Perplexed, Gachelin lowered his head and closed his eyes, pretending, as had become his custom, to pray assiduously.

What on earth was that thing covered with a cloth? he wondered anxiously. Probably another cheap trick from the stunted little visitor.

After what seemed to him to be an eternity, the room was filled with noise again as the assembly rose to its feet.

Abbot Eustache moved quickly on to the second part of the meeting which dealt with the community's accounts and administration. He lingered only on one matter, which might bring Jumièges sizeable tithes, the question of returning Elling Island, which was currently part of the kingdom of England, into the possession of the Norman Abbeys.

'But the Prior will explain all this to you far better than I,' said the Abbot, handing over to Angilbert.

The Prior rose, clinking his heavy gold chain. He moved to the middle of the assembly with an air of great importance.

'The rights of the island should return to Jumièges in their entirety thanks to the intervention of the Pope and the Archbishop of Canterbury. Only one person is still opposed to this move: the Bishop of Winchester, who has the ownership of Elling! This bishop is denying our abbey the transfer, which he himself accorded us a few years ago, therein lies the dispute.'

Eudes, the Rector, raised his hand and, after a nod of approval from the Abbot, began to speak.

'But for goodness sake, if my memory serves me right, he committed himself in the presence of Archbishop Theobald himself, the Archbishop of Canterbury.'

'This is true and now he is asking us to pay him the impressive sum of one hundred silver *markas*!' declared Angilbert, displeased by the interruption.

Oh, if only he were Abbot, he thought resentfully, he would not tolerate such liberties. With him, they would go meekly on their way. The sanctions had been created to be served, after all. Only, there it was, he was not Abbot and every day he found it a little more difficult to bow his head before the weak and ineffectual Eustache. If only the ridiculous little visitor would write a report along those lines for his master!

'One hundred silver *markas*! But we do not have that sort of sum, and it was not in the agreement!' Eudes continued indignantly, oblivious to the Prior's furious expression.

'Calm down, my son, calm down,' Eustache berated him gently. 'God will provide for us. Go on, Brother Prior, we are listening.'

Eudes flushed and sat back down, grumbling to himself. The Prior checked that everyone was concentrating on what he had to say.

'Despite his unfortunate outburst, Brother Eudes is right, this did not appear in the original texts. That is why Archbishop Theobald of Canterbury, the primate of England himself, has given us his word that he will find in our favour.'

A murmur of approval rippled along the rows.

Since Guillaume had been appointed Abbot in 1127, a number of possessions which had been lost during the course of the ferocious Norman wars, had been restored to Jumièges, and it could at last hope to meet its own needs and fulfil its vocational duties as an almsgiver.

The Prior was now silent, eyeing the assembly pointedly, as if the success of this entire negotiation had depended on him alone. Then, arranging the folds of his gold-edged chasuble, which resembled those worn by primates themselves, he regretfully returned to his place amongst his brothers.

Eudes muttered to himself. It was not the first time, but really, this pretentious ass was overstepping the mark. He was taking the credit for work that he alone, as Jumièges's archivist, had carried through. It was he and no one else who had managed to obtain the help of Archbishop Theobald. He who had been working for nearly seven years on this affair entrusted to him by the previous Abbot!

Eudes clenched his fists and said nothing. His hour would come soon enough. He would find some form of revenge for these endless humiliations.

With his big naïve eyes, Odon took in every dissension, every angry gesture, each sign of wounded pride or rancour from the various protagonists. He sighed, thinking how difficult it was for people to forget their flesh and blood, and what a hard task it was to be 'dead to oneself', even for men who sought saintliness . . . or were meant to!

31

The third part of the meeting was about to begin.

The Abbot joined his hands and leant forward to indicate his mood of contemplation.

'Let us pray, brothers, before opening the next chapter.'

An old monk, in the grip of a vicious cough, cleared his throat, and the hall resounded with the sound of monks' feet rubbing and knocking against the wood of their benches. The monks wondered what this chapter might have in store for them, and they kept glancing over towards the altar and the mysterious object that the visitor had put down on it. They were not to be disappointed.

Abbot Eustache came back to stand in front of the lectern, paused for a moment and then announced: 'Some time ago, I read a text by Prior Guigues in the *Consuetudines* of our Chartreux brothers, and I will ask you to meditate on his words because they are very relevant to this meeting:

> *"First take on the mantle –* indue eum prius *– of he whom you would judge and correct, then, do unto him what you would deem to benefit you if you were he."*

The Abbot looked up, there was compassion in his expression, but also something close to fear. Eustache felt the weight of his responsibilities more sorely than ever. He moved forward amongst the monks, declaring in a voice laden with sadness, 'I wish from the very bottom of my heart that one of you would come forward, in confession, and explain to his brothers why he has sinned.'

A murmur rose up from the rows of monks and was quickly stifled.

Gachelin had paled again. Should he denounce himself in public, then? He was hesitating when, quite suddenly, a monk came forward out of the row with an air of determination.

His fellows shuffled and murmured in surprise. They were prepared for anything except for the Precentor, Foulques, to come forward. He turned towards the Abbot and looked up at him with his strange, sad, frog-like features: 'Reverend Father, may I inform you of some facts that . . . that I can no longer keep secret?'

Like all the monks, who were accustomed to observing silence, the burly Precentor was ill at east breaking this rule. His voice was slightly croaky, and he turned his bulging eyes swiftly away from the Abbot, not daring to meet his gaze.

Even though he was amazed by this intervention, Eustache courteously inclined his head to show his acquiescence.

'Go ahead, my brother, go ahead, we are listening.'

The Precentor seemed to gather his thoughts before announcing solemnly, 'Reverend Father, if I have properly understood the meaning of your words and the passage from our holy rules, I believe that it is now my duty to help one of our brothers who is in difficulty.'

His melancholy gaze rested on the Sexton.

'As I was saying, it is my duty to bring one of our beloved brothers back onto the path of righteousness. That is why I would now like to denounce the sinful actions of Brother Gachelin who—'

The Sexton leapt to his feet, dominating the assembly with his impressive height. A nervous tic made his eyelids twitch.

'Silence this man, Reverend Abbot! He knows not what he is saying!'

'Silence!' thundered the Prior.

Everyone was quiet.

'Gachelin, my son, if you have a confession to make to us, we will listen. If not, let Brother Foulques finish what he was saying,' Eustache said beseechingly.

Gachelin let himself drop back onto the bench with his arms crossed and a stubborn expression on his face.

'Continue, Brother Foulques, we are listening,' said the Abbot.

'I thank you, Reverend Father. I was saying that Brother

Gachelin, here present, has committed sins that our community can tolerate no longer, particularly . . . the sin of the flesh!'

This time there was a general furore. Eustache, who had sat down, stood up again to quieten the assembly.

'Father,' he said, turning to face the rotund Precentor, 'this is a most serious accusation. Are you sure of what you are implying?'

Despite the hubbub, Foulques did not falter. He looked at his abbot and said, with a sigh, 'Reverend Father, I am aware of the gravity of my declaration, but I uphold it, especially as I am not the only one in this gathering of brothers who knows the facts. Many of us know about this and have held our tongues for years.'

'Explain yourself,' said the Abbot, stupefied. 'What do you mean, Foulques?'

'Even our Prior, here present, knows about Gachelin's behaviour, not to mention Father Baudri and other officiating monks who shall remain nameless. And as for the villagers, they all know that they have to steer their wives and daughters clear of this man,' he said, pointing accusingly at the Sexton. 'He may well be an oblation, but he still uses his powerful family name to achieve his ends and, if you wish to know everything, even goes so far as paying—'

'It is not true!' shouted the Sexton in a rush of anger. 'This is calumny, Reverend Father, do you hear, lies!'

'By what right, you lowly creature, do you challenge me?' interrupted Prior Angilbert, staring menacingly at Foulques.

'Silence! silence!' said the Abbot who was disturbed by so much agitation. 'That is enough, all of you. Go on, Brother Foulques, please.'

'Not content, as I said, with committing the crime of the flesh, the Sexton has been guilty of stealing the property of the dying and also that of the abbey, Reverend Father!'

'Do you mean that the Sexton stole from us?' asked the Abbot, 'but how?'

'Yes, Reverend, I have reason to believe that he took our sacred relic in order to use it in some base exchange.'

The Abbot raised his hand and declared, 'These accusations are so serious that the man that you accuse must be allowed to explain himself. Brother Gachelin, speak now, because it is surely time. You cannot remain silent.'

The Sexton realised that there was no point in hiding anything any more. He rose to his feet and went to kneel in front of the Abbot.

'Reverend Father,' he said in a voice that shook with anger, 'allow me to confess before you and my brothers. I have sinned, it is true, I have sinned.'

'We are listening, my son,' replied Eustache wearily. 'We are listening. Sit down, all of you, and remain silent, my sons.'

'First of all, I would now like to explain the reasons for my straying from the path of righteousness.'

'Go on, keep going, my child,' the Abbot encouraged gently.

'When I was nine years old, as you may well know, my father, Lord Clères lost his second wife, my mother, whom he loved passionately. The very next day he offered me to the Abbot Guillaume, expelling me from his life, expelling me from my real life, at a time when – already – all I could think of was being dubbed a chevalier.'

A look of silent despair crept over the oblation's features.

'My mother was dead and I was losing everything, I ended up a captive, a prisoner amongst you. Yes,' he went on in a voice that was bitter with emotion, 'I was in a jail! On my soul, I never accepted this. Never, do you hear!'

'Keep calm, my son, and go on.'

'I did not choose this reclusive life as all of you here have done! I wanted to see my father again, to talk things out. I wanted to understand why he had rejected me. For all these years, the only times I have seen him have been during the most important ceremonies at Notre Dame de Jumièges, and even then I had no right to go near him, you were always there to stop me. As I have grown older, I have never ceased to want to escape from this jail in which you hold me. And then time passed, eroding none of my feelings but teaching me to imitate your ways better.'

Gachelin fell silent, reliving his long years of misery. Eustache encouraged him once again.

'Go on, my son, go on.'

'The position of Sexton finally gave me an opportunity to

escape and to return to the world. So I tried to catch up on the years that you stole from me!

'I loved women, many, many women, do you hear? Old and decrepit ones or beautiful virgins, comely married ones or adept whores. I have tasted the flesh of each and every one of them! Taking as much pleasure with the hairless old hags who were grateful for such a gift so late in life, as with the little Venuses who fell into raptures from the very first shudder—'

The Abbot interrupted, his voice trembling with indignation: 'My brother, I should not need to remind you that confession is an act of repentance and humility. You wear our habit and, whether you like it or not, you have taken our vows. Confess with dignity, therefore, or I will be forced to hear your confession in private.'

Gachelin lowered his head with a groan.

'I will try. I have committed the sins of the flesh a thousand times, but I had to find money to fund my lavish tastes and my innumerable women. I rented a house outside the abbey walls so that I could meet my conquests in befitting surroundings.'

'A house – you rented a house?' said the Abbot, stupefied.

'Yes, Reverend Father, and there I have to say that Foulques was right, you must surely be the only one who did not know about it. So, I had a house in which to harbour my loves, eat lavish meals and drink real wine, not the watery Conihout wine which seems to be to your taste, you and my dear brothers! And, I robbed from the dead, not much wrong in that. I made use of what they left behind and, believe me, I made good use of it!'

Without paying any attention to the indignant murmurs that were beginning to spread, Gachelin continued, arrogant to the last.

'Then my father fell ill and my miserly half-brother came and offered me a deal.'

'A deal, you say?'

'He offered me a meeting with my father if I helped him to steal . . .'

The Sexton suddenly hesitated before continuing.

The noise in the assembly rose to a peak. All the monks were talking at once. The Prior had to threaten to send them all out in order to obtain silence.

'Continue, my son,' said Eustache, devastated.

'I wanted to see my father again, so I helped him. It was I who broke the chain to the room where the relics are kept, and I too who stole Saint Philibert's relic . . .'

'But how could you, you did not have the key to the room,' retorted the Abbot.

The Sexton seemed to hesitate and then he said:

'I had stolen the bunch of keys held by the Porter, Tancard . . . he did not even notice, poor old man, and I put the keys back where they belong before he realised they had gone!'

'You think you have been very clever do you not?' interrupted Odon in his fluting little voice. 'So, tell me what your brother Rainolf wanted to do with this.'

And with a rather theatrical gesture, he drew off the cloth that hid the precious reliquary.

Once again the room resounded with the monks' exclamations. Gachelin said nothing, he just stared at the reliquary in astonishment.

Odon went on.

'Did you really think that your charming brother Rainolf would sweetly go and give the relic to your old father. You surprise me!'

'That is what he swore to me on his own head,' muttered Gachelin. 'He said that it would save my father, and that his health would improve, that I could see him again at last. We were going to give the relic back to the abbey afterwards.'

Odon gave a knowing laugh.

'Are you really so naïve? Your brother is very like you, you know, he likes good meat, the ladies and beautiful clothes. Only, you see, these things are expensive and he is burdened with debts, he is desperate. I also think that he was probably weary of seeing your father spending his inheritance coming to the help of churches and an abbey such as this. He, therefore, decided to find his own way of reimbursing himself . . . Did you not know, Brother Gachelin, that he extorted a very high price from your poor father? On top of which, he made another deal and arranged to sell on the precious reliquary to some Italian traders. I have just received the confirmation. They were all waiting impatiently for the poor man to die!'

'You lie!' howled Gachelin, beside himself. 'Our father was dying, my brother would not have dared to ask him for anything; to sell on the relic without telling me about it!'

'Oh yes, he would, he did. And, like a fool, you let yourself be manipulated without even stopping to think.'

Gachelin lowered his head. He realised that he might never see his father alive again, that he had probably only been an instrument in Rainolf's greedy hands.

'It is only by great good fortune,' continued Odon in his gentle voice, 'that others did stop and think and, like the Chevalier de Lesneven, come to the right conclusions. Thanks to de Lesneven, we have been able to reclaim the sacred reliquary before the equinox procession. And now that this matter has been dealt with, let us move on to something else, I am referring to our Father Abbot's seal. Did your brother steal that too?'

'The seal? But, I know nothing about it, have I not confessed enough? I have nothing to do with it.'

'Did you steal it from the Abbot's coffers?' insisted Odon again.

Everyone fell silent. The Abbot, now very pale, did not take his eyes off the Sexton. The latter shook his head but gave no answer to this last accusation. He seemed to have lost interest in the discussion.

'Defend yourself, Gachelin, defend yourself,' begged the Abbot, despite himself.

The Sexton murmured: 'I stole the relic for my father, to see him one last time before he dies . . .'

And suddenly he cried out in the piping voice of the child he had once been, begging, 'I must see him again, Reverend Father, I must see him.'

The Abbot looked down, moved by the man's pain. He realised what he must have gone through, this child given to God by a father who refused to love him.

The voice continued, insistent, pitiful: 'Have pity on me, let me see him, Reverend Father, and I will promise you anything you ask.'

Now this is a strange scene, thought Odon, watching attentively as it developed. Two rows of monks in uproar, their rules forgotten; the Abbot, very pale, prematurely aged, and their sturdy sexton – built like a warrior – begging on bended knee, suddenly talking about his father in the voice of a child.

Brother Odon coughed slightly in an attempt to attract Abbot Eustache's attention.

'Reverend Abbot, may I ask Brother Gachelin a few more questions?'

'Do you think so?' said Eustache wearily. 'Well, if you must!'

Odon went over to the kneeling man and put his hand on his shoulder.

'Brother Gachelin, I would like you to tell us now about your relations with Mistress Edel.'

The Sexton looked up at the young monk, terrified. He shook his head.

'It is one thing,' murmured Odon, 'to be condemned for theft and sins of the flesh by your Abbot, but it is quite another to be condemned for murder by the secular judiciary!'

Gachelin opened his eyes wide.

'Have strength, we are listening,' ordered Odon keeping a firm hold on the Sexton's shoulder.

'What do you want to know?' asked the monk in a hesitant voice, looking straight ahead.

'What your relationship with her was,' replied the little monk curtly.

'I fell in love and . . .'

'And?'

'And I became her lover,' whispered Gachelin.

'Where were you on the night when she suffered her terrible death?'

'Are you accusing me of that too? No, I loved her, I did . . . Oh, Edel . . . I loved her, do you hear!'

Gachelin had leapt to his feet, and stood facing the young monk.

'Answer my question, then.'

'I was with Rainolf, my half-brother. She was killed on the night that we stole the relic, after the revelries. Afterwards I went back to bed in the common dorter.'

'Did anyone see you?'

'No, I think not,' hesitated the Sexton.

'You think not, or you are sure?'

'Well, I would not want to denounce anyone. Perhaps the person that I met would like to come forward to confirm that I was going back to my place in the dorter.'

There was a long silence. The Prior came forward.

'I did, in fact, meet Gachelin when he was going back to bed, as I was. I could not sleep and was coming back from the monastic gardens where I had been sitting under the arches for quite a while.'

'There, you see. And, anyway, I could not have killed her, she was the only one – out of all of them – the only one that I cared for . . . For pity's sake, Reverend Father, believe me.'

The Sexton threw himself to his knees in front of the Abbot once more, grabbing the hem of his chasuble, kissing his feet. The Abbot stepped back, very pale.

'Enough, my brother. Get up and go back to your place. I declare this chapter closed.'

'But . . .' Odon protested gently. 'There is still so much to clear up, Reverend Father.'

'What more is there?'

'There is, Reverend Father, the death of a brother, which everyone here seems to have forgotten.'

The Abbot frowned, apparently exasperated.

'What do you mean, Brother Odon?'

'I mean the Under-Sexton, Joce, who is never mentioned here any more except on the roll of the dead!'

The little monk swept the entire assembly with his candid eye and declared coolly: 'Yes, my brothers, I need another confession. It would be good if the man who killed Joce, denounced himself.'

'I did not kill him,' protested a hoarse voice.

A strongly built monk had risen to his feet to come forward a few paces. Every trace of irony fled from his expression, leaving only fear.

'Father Baudri!' exclaimed the Abbot Eustache, stunned.

The Father Hosteller looked down at the floor. Over the last few days everyone had noticed how much his mood had changed.

He knelt in front of the Abbot and murmured: 'I did not kill Joce, my father. Joce is—'

'Are you quite sure?' interrupted Odon. 'And yet you are here before God the only man responsible for his death, Father Baudri.'

The Father Hosteller threw a terrified glance at the little monk, he had underestimated him. Then he retorted, 'By what right do you say such a thing and, anyway, what can you know about what really happened between Joce and myself?'

'Much more than you would wish. Just as with the relic, Chevalier Galeran was a great help to me. He made his enquiries and, thanks to him, I knew what happened in Duclair. I knew what sort of man was hiding behind this affable façade—'

'Enough,' the Hosteller cried out, getting to his feet, his face suddenly ashen. 'Enough, do you hear! Make him stop, Reverend Father!'

'Nay no, Baudri, I have not finished and my name is not Joce the Fear. It takes more than your anger and your blows to keep me quiet, you know!'

Running his hands through his short red beard all the while, Odon stood and stared at the man in front of him.

'This is all my business and mine alone,' protested Baudri, so quietly that Odon could hardly hear him.

'Except that you ceased to belong to yourself on the day that you became a member of this community, Baudri. Had you forgotten this . . . ?' said Odon, taking a vellum from his purse and showing it to the Father Hosteller. 'This deed, signed by your hand and placed on the sacred altar, this profession of faith in which you committed yourself to serving God.'

Discomfited, Baudri looked down and pleaded:

'I did not kill him! In the name of God, I did not kill him, I swear it.'

'As a child,' continued Odon as if he had heard nothing, 'Joce became your whipping boy. He was ten years younger than you, the slave who executed all your orders, who lived in fear of you. Because, just as you have done here, you hid beneath your pleasant outward appearance a cruel and violent nature, which only Joce knew about. He had suffered so much at your hands that he became generally known as Joce *le Péor*. He was even afraid, as you told the chevalier when he first arrived, of his own shadow. And his shadow was you, Baudri!'

The Hosteller no longer had anything to say, he had fallen to his knees again at the Abbot's feet, and the latter was looking at him, stupefied.

Implacable, Odon went on.

'One day, Joce disappeared without a trace, fleeing his home . . . fleeing from you. And you looked for him everywhere! And then, by chance, you discovered that he had taken refuge here in Jumièges. And suddenly you too wanted to take your vows!'

Baudri gave no reply, he was sitting back on his heels, staring blankly ahead.

'Time passed and you became the Father Hosteller. But there was a problem, Joce was no longer your slave. He was under Gachelin's orders and you could not tolerate that! Many a time you engineered events to try and retrieve him, without any success. Gachelin valued his assistant, especially as he was able to get him to do all the work. So, you started to hate Gachelin, to take an interest in his little schemes, to understand his weaknesses . . .'

'I did not kill him,' whispered Baudri breathlessly.

'And you could only think of one thing, ridding yourself of Gachelin so that you might take Joce back! The Bishop of Lisieux received a series of briefs, most of which came from you. In them you denounced the poor conduct within the monastery and even reporting – you must have overheard some compromising conversation between Gachelin and his brother – the theft of the relic.'

'It is not true,' protested Baudri feebly.

'Oh but it is! I compared your writing to the writing on some of the parchments sent to the Bishop, and it is certainly yours, my brother. Then one day—'

'Be quiet, stop,' begged the Hosteller.

'One day,' the little monk went on in his soft voice, 'you arranged to meet Joce next to the fish ponds . . . it was on the evening of the great whale hunt. What went on between the two of you that evening? Did your slave rebel for the first time in his sorry life? In any event, you seized him by the neck and you squeezed, and squeezed—'

'No! No! I just wanted to frighten him, believe me. He . . . he went completely white . . . and then, he fell into the pond before I could stop him. He was dead when I got him out, it is the truth!'

'Yes, Joce died of fear, and Chevalier de Lesneven understood that long before I did,' murmured Odon. 'But you alone are responsible, Baudri. And, if you were innocent, why did you not bring him back to the abbey, and confess to the Abbot? Instead you threw him into the Seine, hoping everyone would believe it was an accidental death! Then you told Gachelin to ring in Nocturn, and when I questioned you in the monastic gardens, you were so innocent that the only thing you wanted to do was to appease your hatred by loading all suspicion onto the Sexton and his family!'

The man had slumped down. He was no longer even trying to protest.

'So you see, my brother, still there is something in all this that I do not understand, something unbelievable!'

Odon fell silent. Standing with his eyes closed, the little monk seemed to be in pain, as if he were waiting for inspiration to come from elsewhere. Everyone was watching him. There was an interminable silence and then, finally, Odon opened his eyes again and started to speak once more.

'My brother, your confession seems to me to be very incomplete. It is not our place to probe every body and each heart, we are all fallible and damaged, we all suffer and cause suffering . . .'

The Father Hosteller glanced at him anxiously.

'But really, this master-slave relationship, these beatings, this violence, this so-called fatal accident . . . and, yet, you became a monk to be with him, abandoning everything for him! And that makes me start asking questions.'

Baudri had turned to his inquisitor, his face ashen.

'What then was the exact nature of your relationship with poor Joce, Father Baudri?'

The Abbot opened his eyes wide: as he had listened to the little monk's revelations, he too had begun to wonder . . . a quick glance at the monk's tortured face left him in no doubt, he stood up.

'Answer, my brother, I order you to answer!'

Baudri wiped his brow and stammered: 'Have I not admitted enough?'

'If you do not want to reply, I will reply for you,' said Odon implacably.

Baudri lowered his head obstinately, Odon continued.

'There is only one explanation for the perversity and the violence of your relationship with Joce and that is a guilty passion!'

Horrified murmurings echoed around the room.

'If the truth be known, you followed the unfortunate Brother Joce all the way to this abbey because you were never able to suppress the passion that you felt for him! The passion of a mature man for a younger man, a weak and gentle boy like to a maiden. A boy who was terrified by your violence, who had to put up with everything from you, even the unthinkable! Because Joce never loved you, Baudri, and that was your undoing. Joce lived in fear and gave you what you wanted in order to avoid the violent punishments you had visited on him since he was a child.'

Hearing these words, the Hosteller let out a searing cry.

'A fear, as I was saying, that devoured him and drove him away from Duclair to escape from you! The elderly still talk about you there, Baudri. They have not forgotten anything of the man that you were.'

The monk shook his head and protested feebly: 'And I loved him so much . . .'

'Oh yes, you loved him! To the extent that you looked for him for years. And then you started a new life in Caudebec, if I am to believe the records kept by Rector Eudes. Unfortunately, fate allowed you to discover that Joce was at Jumièges and your unhealthy passion gripped you once more as it had on the very first day. I cannot guess how long you may have hesitated, but once again you abandoned everything to find him. So you had to become a monk? Well, you did not let even that stand in your way!'

The incredulous monks were speechless, eager to hear what was coming next. The Abbot, sitting uneasily in his imposing sedilia, looked on in irritation.

Odon continued: 'The fish ponds are in a secluded place,

hidden by screens of vegetation. A place people like to meet, away from the public gaze. Because he was accustomed to obeying you, Joce followed you there . . . But what made you suddenly so angry, what drove you to the brutal act which, this time, would bring about our brother's death? What you attempted, Father Baudri, goes by an ugly name, and that name is rape!'

Baudri cried out: 'No! No! He . . . he no longer wanted me. He said he would rather die. He wanted to denounce me to the Abbot. Me! who had always loved him! I just wanted to frighten him so that he would not leave me on my own, but I swear, in the name of God, that I did not want him dead! He died of fear, of fear, do you not see! I loved him so much, do you understand? I have only ever loved him . . .'

And the great monk howled like a wild animal, a grimace of agony twisting his features. The chapter house fell silent. The monks, appalled, could not speak a word.

Baudri collapsed face down, with his arms stretched out forming a cross. He lay on the ground, racked by sobs. Odon did not even seem to notice.

'Poor Joce, he was afraid of everything but that day he dared to resist you and he died as a result . . . like a martyr. I will not add another word, any decisions lie in the hands of Father Abbot.'

Eustache rose to his feet suddenly.

'The chapter is closed,' he declared curtly.

'But no, Father—' protested Odon.

'Did you not hear, Brother? The chapter is concluded,' cut in the Abbot abruptly, and, turning towards the monks, he added: 'You will all – and that includes you Gachelin and you Baudri – follow the procession and pray that God may forgive you for not being worthy of his commandments. Foulques, I will hold you personally responsible, as I will you, Angilbert, for the safety of the Sexton and for his behaviour outside the abbey walls. Baudri, from now on you will be under guard of the Cellarer, Onfroi, and I expect you to do your best to do your duty at this time of great difficulty!'

The Prior glowered furiously at the Precentor. Only the Sexton, lost in terrible thought, seemed indifferent to his fate.

Baudri did not move. The Abbot gave a signal to two monks who took him by the armpits, forcing him to get up.

'We will wait until the chapter tomorrow to deliberate,' continued the Abbot. 'You, you and you, take the sacred relic down to the treasure room. Brother Eudes, go with them and prepare the litter for the procession. My brothers, I am depending on your contemplation. Go in peace!'

The Reverend Father left the chapter house, walking gloomily between the two rows of monks who bowed as he passed. Odon noted, with interest, Angilbert and Foulques's exasperated gesticulations as they pushed the Sexton towards the door, and he thought to himself that the Abbot had not put that particular threesome together by chance.

The assembly dispersed amid the noise of wood grating on flagstones as the benches were pushed back. There was very little time left before the great procession was to begin.

32

After the assembly during which, once again, nothing had been decided, Odon followed Abbot Eustache all the way to his cell. He had not been invited to do so, but he did not let that deter him. He closed the door carefully behind him.

The Abbot had gone over to the window and was staring into the distance with his arms crossed, remaining obstinately silent.

'You certainly are carrying a heavy burden of responsibility, Father,' said Odon eventually, having taken the liberty of sitting down.

Eustache turned round, visibly surprised by the monk's tone of voice.

'What do you mean by that? If you have something to say to me, then do so, and then leave me in peace, I do not have time enough on my hands to waste it!'

'But we shall not waste it, you'll see, Father. First of all, sit down, I want to tell you a story.'

'A story! A story! But, upon my word, have you lost your mind?' said the Abbot, staring at him.

'I think not, Father. Sit down, please.'

He obeyed with a begrudging smile. This little monk's nerve really did know no limits.

'Good, that is better,' said Odon. 'Now, I shall tell you a very old story . . . a story which goes back, if I'm not mistaken, to the year 594.

'In that year Théodoline offered a crown to her husband, the Duke of Turin, but it was not just any crown because it was made of a circle of iron covered in fine gold leaf. It was in fact a sacred crown because, in her great wisdom, Théodoline wanted to show the Duke that the power that everyone so coveted shone with a deceitful light. That it is actually a very heavy and sometimes unbearable burden for whoever wields it . . .'

'In other words, Brother Odon, I can tell you nothing that you do not already know. You are too clever,' said the Abbot impatiently.

'I know what I know,' went on the little monk affably, 'as a child knows what it knows, that is the extent of my gift!'

'And so?'

'And so, Father Abbot, I know that you despise the responsibility that has been entrusted to you. In spite of yourself, you now wear the iron crown and it has never deceived you with its golden gleam. You were the descendant of a powerful family and yet you came and hid yourself humbly in a monastery. At the same time you renounced a great fortune in order to live a life of poverty and, above all, obedience.

'I think that, even then, you knew your weakness and your ineptitude for governing. I would go so far as to say that you came here to escape any form of responsibility and not out of vocation or devotion to our Lord!'

For a moment Odon thought the Abbot might faint. After a moment's hesitation he went on.

'Providence played a trick on you. Because in this monastery, as everywhere on this lowly earth, there is a fierce struggle for power. You are simply the victim of particularly perverse machinations.

'Some people here do, in fact, know your background only too well. They brought you to power precisely because they knew you were incapable of exercising it! To them you were just a puppet. They scored points for each of your mistakes and weak decisions. Not only were they laughing in the face of our sacred law, but some of them were sending successions of denunciations to His Grace the Bishop of Lisieux, thinking that they would then be able to supplant you and accede to the top rung of the hierarchy, to posts that had hitherto been beyond their grasp . . . They probably even had their eye on Lisieux! I shall not name them, you know who I mean.'

'In your eyes, then, I am guilty . . . of weakness?' asked the Abbot nervously.

'It is not for me to judge, these men found a way of using our laws with malign intent in order to reach their own ends, but you, you did not find in yourself the strength to counter their manoeuvres. Worse still, because of your inertia, you have favoured them, you have encouraged this den of iniquity.'

'I was so alone,' said the Abbot sadly.

'That is what the crown of iron is like,' murmured Odon, 'but when a father no longer controls his sons, the wise scriptures say, then they deny themselves nothing, no forbidden sweetmeats, no shameful thoughts . . . and, soon enough, not even murder.'

'What should I do then, what would you advise?' asked the Abbot who was more and more disturbed by Odon's words.

'Cover your head with the ash of repentance, and go barefoot to His Grace in Lisieux to confess your weakness and your ineptitude. But that in itself will obviously call for a measure of courage, you have always found it easier to let everything go . . . And now, Father, give me the seal. I hope that you have not destroyed it.'

The other man looked at him in amazement.

'How did you know?'

'Because it was the only possible explanation. It was you, and only you, who spirited it away, was it not?'

The Abbot did not reply.

'You made it disappear,' said Odon sharply, 'because that way you could reject the iron crown, become a king genuinely without power. Now, go and get the seal, Jumièges will not survive without it.'

Without a word, the Abbot Eustache went to his cot and took something small from under the mattress. He sent it spinning onto the table so violently that it fell to the ground.

Odon bent down, picked up the seal respectfully, wiped it with the back of his sleeve and put it back on the table, saying in a mollifying tone: 'Look at that, it happens to us all does it not, forgetting where we have put something!'

He turned on his heel and went out, leaving the Abbot speechless.

33

Brother Odon felt light-hearted as he came out of the Abbot's cell.

'How did I manage that, tell me Holy Mother?' he murmured. 'No, it was not I, it was you who showed me the way and gave me so much courage today.'

It had to be said that, though Odon revered God, it was the Virgin Mary, the gentle mother of Christ, he felt was his constant companion. Perhaps because his own mother had done little more for him than bringing him into the world in troubled times, Mary and the angels had become the little monk's family, those who tirelessly gave him signs of their discreet love. Sometimes, to his considerable confusion, he found when he conversed with them that his feet seemed to leave the ground, so great was his longing to be united with his celestial friends.

An abrupt shock brought Odon back to earth. Having just turned a corner in the corridor he bumped straight into an ageing brother who moved away, muttering, 'That's the last thing we need now, flying monks!'

34

Hundreds of pilgrims, most of whom had travelled great distances, were converging on Jumieges. Many of them had arrived the day before and had slept beneath the abbey walls. At the first light of dawn, they folded up their blankets and their bundles of belongings. They warmed themselves in groups round meagre fires as they waited eagerly for the ostentatious procession of the sacred relic.

The monastery bells started pealing out and at last the litter appeared, carried by four sturdy monks. They held it up on outstretched arms so that everyone could see the dazzling reliquary, gleaming on a bed of flowers.

The crowd came to life immediately with cries of exaltation and reverential chanting. A group of monks ran on ahead to part the crowd, make room and organise the procession.

The Abbot walked at the procession's head, preceded by children enthusiastically ringing bells, and he blessed the pilgrims and peasants who prostrated themselves as he passed.

The monks made their way down the white track chanting. As a sign of their humility, they walked barefoot and with their heads uncovered. The villagers followed them with their hands joined in prayer, devotedly repeating the monks' words. They were sure in their hearts that Saint Philibert would save them from the storm and the ruination it could bring.

Led by the Abbot Eustache, the long procession came into the village square where it stopped on a carpet of flowers. The windows of the cottages were hung with sheets of cloth and wool decorated with garlands of leaves. A hushed silence descended and the elders of the village, led by Drogtegand, came to kneel before the Abbot who lifted each one back to his feet, drawing the sign of the cross on his forehead.

Some of the pilgrims were pushing and jostling to get close to Saint Philibert's relic, and to touch it. A few of the children were so overexcited that they ran aimlessly in all directions, screaming shrilly.

Having blessed each house as he passed it, the Abbot took the track that led to the river, to the place where the ceremony was held.

It was at this moment that the chevalier arrived, bringing little Mabille home. He had to stop his steed to let the long procession of monks and the faithful pass by, and he crossed himself as the sacred reliquary came past.

Before he was canonised, Philibert had been a very just and tenacious man; his family was from Gascony, just like the chevalier's mother. This thought made him smile, and he felt that the saint would be with him in his search for the murderer.

In the confusion and bustle around them, people were beginning to stare in amazement and tongues were beginning to wag: 'It is Mabille! Look, on the chevalier's horse! Yes, look, it is her, I told you!'

Mabille had changed so much that the villagers did not immediately recognise her. She was pale and looked like a young lady from the town with her shoes and her Rouen shawl.

She herself, conscious of so many eyes locked onto her and a little afraid, in spite of everything, clung to the chevalier who held her to him a little more tightly.

'It is all right, little one, everything will be all right,' said Galeran, feeling her tense.

The chevalier's voice was so calm that Mabille tilted her little chin up again and proudly draped herself in her beautiful shawl, facing up to the inquisitive stares of the villagers that surrounded them.

One man, hidden in the crowd, did not take his eyes off her. He screwed up his eyes, watching her every move. He had found her at last, and to think that he had almost missed her in her smart new clothes. Luckily, despite the bustle, a couple on horseback always catches the eye.

He smiled as he looked automatically at his hands, and then his smile faded, and he rubbed his palms together vigorously, trying to erase the splashes of blood that he alone could see, stains that would not go away.

She would have to be silenced too. All he had to do was follow her. The confounded chevalier would not be by her side for ever. He had made up his mind, he would kill her. She had to die, he thought with a little private laugh, as he wiped his hands on his hose. But the other one first, the other one had to go first. It was so easy. It was all so easy . . . .

The chevalier could feel that Mabille was shivering.

'What is the matter, Mabille?' he asked.

'I know not, my Lord, I feel vexed, as if there were something evil here,' she said indicating the swelling crowd anxiously.

'Do not be afraid, little one. This great crowd and all this noise are bound to upset you. We shall soon be able to get across,' said the chevalier to reassure her.

But he too felt uncomfortable. He knew that little alarm signal only too well, that little shiver of danger. In these sort of situations, he knew it was best to obey his instincts. He kicked Quolibet on and cutting through the crowd, which parted quickly before the horse, cantered towards the end of the village where Mabille's family would be waiting.

For a moment he wondered whether he might be wrong to be taking her home, far from the protection of the monks and Lady Frédesande, but rejected this idea forcefully. It had to be done. Now, he was quite sure, the evil beast who had killed Edel would come out of hiding . . .

35

The Abbot led the procession to the port of Jumièges where he stopped, watching the to-ing and fro-ing of little boats, and the increasing turbulence of the Seine.

Some boats, laden with passengers and gifts for the abbey, drew alongside. The river's gently sloping banks were scattered with cages full of ducks and chickens, casks of wine, a ewe, sacks of flour, salt, bread, cheeses, hundreds of flowers . . . all in offering to Saint Philibert.

Square-sailed sailing boats from Caudebec were tacking towards the shore to get closer and greet the procession. On the eve of the equinox everyone came to ask for help from the patron saint of Jumièges.

Abbot Eustache gestured for the reliquary to come over to him. The four monks carrying the litter made their way through the crowd, which parted unwillingly to let them pass.

The Reverend Abbot walked down onto the sandy edge of the river and, lifting the hem of his chasuble, walked several paces into the water. The monks, lifting the litter onto their strong shoulders, followed him into the current. On a sign from the Prior, who had turned to face the crowd, everyone kneeled and fell silent.

On the far bank, the onlookers bowed their heads. The rippling waves surged towards the bank and subsided.

In its perfect stillness, there was something magical about that moment. Standing squarely in the river, the praying monks beseeched their patron saint to calm the fury of the equinox tide.

The Abbot was still looking straight ahead over the brilliant gleaming reliquary to the dark waters of the great river and the silhouettes of the people kneeling at the foot of the tall cliffs.

He smiled, then intoned an *Ave Maria*, which was taken up enthusiastically by the ardent crowd.

After a brief prayer, in which the Abbot asked Saint Philibert to grant his protection on the Terre Gémétique and its inhabitants, the Abbot gathered his thoughts for a moment. Then, with a sweeping movement of his hand, he blessed the great river once more.

'Help yourself and heaven will help you!' thought the villagers before they dispersed because, on this equinox eve, they had much to do. As if on a ship that is heading into a storm, they had to secure the village's defences.

On the other bank, the inhabitants of Heurteauville, which was regularly flooded, had barricaded their houses and put their family coffers where the water could not reach them. Most of them would spend that night in the hamlet of Jumièges, or would climb up towards the abbey.

The waters of the Seine were already very turbulent and sharp little waves slapped violently against the jetty. In spite of this, people were queuing for the ferry on the left bank of the river, to get over to the peninsula. Even the fishermen were using their boats to ferry across local families and the last of the pilgrims who had come from Bec Hellouin, Lisieux or from Pont-Audemer . . .

The shepherds, who had left Heurteauville early that morning, were leading their flocks to safety, to the meadows around the tithe-barn in which the animals would be shut up for the day while the storm raged.

In Jumièges, the villagers built up banks of earth around their houses with the help of visitors from Conihout. Men used fishing nets to lash down the roofs of those cottages that were most exposed to the wind. Planks of wood were positioned across doorsteps to dam the rising waters. So violent was the equinox storm that every kind of precaution had to be taken in the windy days leading up to it.

36

As if in a dream, Rurik heard the bells of Jumièges ringing out midnight in the distance.

He was standing under cover of the trees at the edge of the forest. It was a clear night and just a couple of hundred paces away he could make out the long façade of the isolated building. After three nights of running through the woods, he had to make use of what was left of his strength and will just to stay on his feet.

Finally, he made up his mind and in a few strides he reached the holly copse which stood between the great house and the deserted road. Once there, he crouched behind the spiky bushes with his weapon lying across his knees, and he rested a while.

He knew that he should have got to Caudebec or the safety of the abbey a long time ago. This was the perfect moment. Despite the strong wind, a thick fog hung stagnantly over the Seine and its neighbouring swamps. The village was thronging with pilgrims and, unusually, everyone was coming and going without paying much attention to who else was about.

Nevertheless, an irresistible desire consumed the young Dane and forced him, despite himself, towards this large solitary house. His hands tensed on his weapon. He knew that if the locals saw him in open ground and managed to catch him, there would be no judgement, no explanation, just a horrible death, a death as horrible as poor Edel's . . . And if that were to happen, that would be the end of it and her assassin would be satisfied, he would go on living quite peacefully.

'Immortal God,' sobbed Rurik, 'What misfortune I have borne in these few days, what pain! I have started to loathe the one that I loved . . . No, I lie, that is not true, I still love her, as if her horrible death forced me too, in spite of myself.'

He strained his ears, looked around, hesitated a little longer, then leapt quickly into the shadow of the old house.

There, he ran along the wall, turned down the left-hand side of the house and came to a low window, with a closed wooden shutter. Holding his breath, he put his eye right up to a gap in the shutter. Everything was quiet and he could see no light at all inside.

He very quickly sprang the lock on the inside with his knife. Then he pushed open the shutter, stepped through the window and was inside the house.

For a fleeting moment he thought he was dreaming again, that Edel's warm arms would reach out for him, that he would hug her so forcefully to him that she could barely breathe and that, as always, she would escape, slithering away like an eel, making promises she would never keep.

Rurik came to his senses and studied the dark room. He went unsteadily over to the back of the room, where there was a curtained bed, Edel's bed.

He pulled the curtain aside and suddenly started to tremble from head to foot. In front of him, under the thick cover, a small form was sleeping and he realised to his terror that she was breathing.

Rurik sighed deeply, his eyes rolled back in his head and he fell, full length, on the floor.

37

When he regained consciousness, Rurik was still stretched out on the floor. By the light of a candle, he saw an anxious little face bending over him.

'Mabille! But what are you doing here?' he murmured, lifting himself up onto his elbow.

The girl leapt backwards and Rurik let himself fall back to the ground.

'Mabille, I swear to you, you must not fear me! I am innocent of everything with which I am charged, please, you must believe me . . . ! Do you not know me, do you not know how much I loved Edel?'

The girl had moved closer to him like a wary little animal.

'That is just why,' she said in a whisper, 'it is because you loved her so.'

'Do we hurt those we love, then?'

Mabille shook her head nervously. Then she rallied thinking of the goodly Lady Frédesande, who was so helpful and compassionate.

'Firstly, do not talk so loudly,' she said. 'Do you want people to hear you? And you must rest because you are in a terrible state!'

She helped him as best she could to drag himself onto the bed, the bed in which he had so longed to lie with Edel.

His features wore an expression of profound distress and suddenly his cheeks were streaming with tears of pain and exhaustion.

Mabille felt her heart go out to him, she took the young Dane's hand and squeezed it with all her might.

'I am sure you could not have done it, not for anything in the world!' she murmured.

Her soft, sweet voice got the better of Rurik's last shred of resistance. He closed his eyes and his features relaxed as he sank into a deep sleep.

By the feeble light of the candle, Mabille studied his handsome face at her leisure as it glowed with sweat and tears.

'He looks like a statue,' she said to herself, 'a sleeping statue.'

She stretched her hand out to his long fair hair. It was strange, she thought, that it should be so soft, as soft as her own or her little brother's.

'It is as if he were mine,' she murmured. And then added with more conviction: 'You are mine!'

PART FIVE

'Like the banks of a pond,
the gloomy hem of a cloud,
Like a black autumn night,
or a dark winter's day,
My thoughts are darker still
than a black autumn night!'

The Kalevala,
popular Finnish epic

38

The long-dreaded day of the equinox arrived. All the way from the mouth of the river to the good town of Rouen, scores of watchmen, with their horns strapped across their shoulders, had posted themselves to watch the movements of the waters and the colour of the skies.

That morning great layers of fog still lay heavily over the marshes and the peculiarly still waters. Then all of a sudden, and this speed was itself a sign of foreboding, a strong westerly whipped up, driving away the last of the mist, lifting spirals of sand and dust, and sweeping past the tops of the tallest trees.

Above the watchmen's heads, tumbling and disordered like a dark noisy living cloak, flew hundreds of birds, herons, teals, seagulls, crows, fleeing to seek refuge further inland.

Sitting cross-legged on a rocky promontory, Drogtegand watched sternly. A young farm labourer, with his horn in his hand, stood by his side awaiting the signal. The old man furrowed his brow: the shape of the clouds, the wind and the direction taken by the birds augured no good.

Flights of wild ducks suddenly rose up from the marshes and, after describing a wide circle over the abbey, headed south.

Drogtegand understood that this tide would not be like others, the ducks knew that and, instead of heading for Rouen, had chosen to go towards Ouche. On the old man's signal, the younger man beside him put his horn to his mouth and, filling his lungs with air, sent an echoing call towards the hamlet.

Heavy clouds, driven on by the north wind, were unfurling over the Terre Gémétique. Drogtegand screwed up his eyes. The sky, which had been pale yellow when he woke, was going grey, a dull, dirty grey like window lead.

He stood up quickly, leaving the young watchman to his

work. He had to get back to the hamlet and make sure that everyone was evacuated. These warning signs did little to please him, it reminded him too clearly of the terrible year in the days of the Abbot Guillaume when the equinox tide had swallowed up part of Conihout and Heurteauville, flooding the hamlet of Jumièges and drowning a number of men and beasts.

'Of course,' thought the elder as he made his way to the village, 'since then we have built earth banks round the village, and the dykes at Conihout and Heurteauville, but will they stand up to such a great tide?'

As if to confirm his fears, the warning call from the horns in Caudebec carried to him on the wind, along with the furious ringing of the tocsin in Saint-Wandrille.

The alarm had been sounded, and the bells of Jumièges swung into action, relaying the signal of the storm so that it was carried from church to church all the way to the city of Rouen, and to its cathedral.

The course of fate had been set. Men nailed the last planks to the windows and doors of their cottages. Everything that could be tied down was tied down. The boats had been heaved up to the little beech wood and tightly bound to the tree trunks.

Terce had not yet been rung in when streams of women, children and the elderly, laden with their few belongings, made their way to the abbey to seek refuge. The peasants' faces were dark. Even the children, who were usually so noisy, were frightened and kept quiet, clinging to their mothers' hands.

Every year all the inhabitants of the Terre Gémétique suffered the ravages of the great tides, but it was always nothing compared to the terrible stories related to them by the very old.

As he strode forward more rapidly, Drogtegand remembered the evenings on watch when the villagers all gathered in the main square, throwing a few dry logs onto the fire and tirelessly listening to the harsh voice of old Gaitelgrime, the blind story-teller from Conihout.

'Listen. Listen now,' the old woman would say as the flames lit up her milky eyes, 'to the ancient story of the tides. Listen to the story that our ancestors and their ancestors before them used to tell, because perhaps some day, or some night, the tide will come to get you, you and those you love . . . just as it did me.'

Gaitelgrime pointed her thin straight finger at them, and the peasants crossed themselves and moved swiftly aside so as not to be the subject of the blind old woman's pointings. Even the young men gulped and the women huddled close to their men, while the old woman continued her tales, a smile playing on her dry lips.

'In those days,' said Gaitelgrime, 'the waters came and beat upon the walls of the abbey. It was in the time of the dragon boats and the treacherous people. A time of storms and of fear!'

Gaitelgrime stopped, sweeping her white-eyed gaze over her audience as if she were looking for someone; perhaps she was looking for her husband and her son who had been swept away by the great tide forty years before.

The old woman shook her head, spitting on the ground acrimoniously, and she spat out her words too.

'That year, plenty of the very old and the very young had been carried off by famine.

'And then a great whale came. He was so big that the towers of Jumièges looked small beside him. The men hunted him and caught him . . . but he killed many of them before he was finally cut with the iron blade. The exhausted Leviathan bore all the anger of the sea in his flesh and he rotted before we could even eat him!

'The stench of his entrails hung over the village but that was still not the end of it that accursed year, because the Leviathan was a warning from the great tide, the fifty year tide!'

The villagers huddled closer and closer together as they stood warming their hands by the fire. When Gaitelgrime was telling her stories, even the flames felt cold, and great shivers shook them all.

'That year the winds had blown so, and so they had blown, that the frenzied sea had risen up like a great wall of green, a wall so tall that no one had ever seen anything like it! The cliffs remember it to this day . . . The wave destroyed everything in its path and then – right in front of Jumièges – it met our river. The impact was terrible to behold and the mingled waters sprang up to a great height. It was the highest tide anyone had ever seen, and few lived to tell the tale . . .

'Whole flocks disappeared in their entirety, snatched by the waters. A tall ship which was heading for the port of Rouen was cleft in two as if by a mighty axe. And the forest, even the deep, distant forest, was completely submerged! The fish were flitting through the branches instead of birds, the world was turned upside down with water everywhere and air underneath.'

The audience listened breathlessly. The old woman rubbed her hands together as if she were now cold, and then, rocking backwards and forward on her feet, she went on in a voice still more hoarse.

'The waves had gone beyond the walls of Jumièges and they would have swallowed up the abbey itself if the good Lord had not watched over it. In the village, on the other hand . . . every woman, every child, the old and infirm, they had died, drowned, their mutilated bodies swept away by the water . . .'

Drogtegand sighed, this story reminded him too much of the succession of bad omens in recent days: the death of the whale hunters, and of Joce and poor Edel . . . And then the terrible north wind, which was now blowing so hard that you had to lean against it to walk into it.

Gaitelgrime might be right; they would all die sooner or later, perhaps swept away by the tide.

The old man shook his head, disappointed in himself, and picked up a little girl who had tripped over beside him, pushing her gently back towards her mother who was too heavily laden to hold on to her child.

He made his way over towards the houses, checking over the last minute work, asking the men to nail back down the occasional door or shutter that was poorly attached, re-tying a knot that was not holding. He checked the attachments of the nets over the roofs and chivvied a young man who could not think how to begin evacuating his wife, newly delivered of a baby boy.

39

When Rurik woke up, he looked around without really under-
standing where he was. Weak sunlight filtered through the
shutter at the only window. The room was empty and quite
silent. Memories of the last few days gradually came back to
him, terrifying visions that belonged in a nightmare . . . But no,
it is the truth, it really has happened, he told himself, and the
truth is like a harpoon that has been unleashed and no one can
do anything to stop.

The young man stretched his aching limbs and stood up
painfully.

'I have caught myself in my own trap,' he thought. 'I
must run away, or the others are going to cut me down like a
flower.'

Then the thought of Mabille suddenly struck him, where had
she gone, could he trust her?

On the table, not far from him, he saw a pitcher and a parcel
tied up in white cloth. He opened it and found bread, ham and a
little round cheese wrapped in straw.

He realised that he was appallingly hungry and he sat at the
table and tore at the food, which disappeared in the twinkling
of an eye.

Then he went over to the basin full of water standing on a
trestle by the window. He wrenched off his torn tunic and then
peeled off what was left of the moss and grasses that still stuck to
his wounds. He had just started to wash when Mabille came into
the room.

Rurik turned to face her and they stood looking at each other
in silence for a long time.

Eventually, the Dane said shakily: 'Mabille, can you tell me
what all this means, and why you behave as if you were at home
here?'

The girl smiled at him prettily and it reminded him of the not too distant past when he had believed he was happy and invincible.

'Here,' she said, handing him a clean tunic, 'it used to belong to Edel's uncle, when he was still in this world. It should be about your size!'

She calmly went and sat down on a stool and he carried on talking as he put on the clean tunic with obvious pleasure.

'And look at you, dressed up like a princess, and you never even used to have shoes on your feet!'

Mabille replied slowly, forcing herself to master the tremor in her voice: 'And why should a poor labourer's daughter not have the right to be properly dressed?'

'No, no,' said Rurik quickly, 'forgive me, you know that you are very pretty dressed as you are.'

'Was I so terribly ugly before, then?'

The young Dane looked down, not knowing what to say next. He grumbled playfully: 'You women and your sharp tongues!'

Mabille felt flattered, he thought of her as a woman then. That was certainly the first time that anyone had thought of her as anything more than a girl.

'Right,' she said rather importantly, 'it is really very simple. First of all, I was ill and the monks kept me at the sanatorium, then the chevalier took me back to my family. Then the chevalier said that Edel's aunt, who can do nothing for herself, could not live on her own in this big house so far from everything, and that it would be a good idea if I looked after her, and that it would bring in some money for my family. I was pleased because Aunt Arda is very kind. She can hardly walk now, and she is totally deaf but she has very good eyesight and she embroiders things for priests and to make decorations for sacred places. She even said that, if I wanted, she would teach me to do it because Edel was not really interested . . . Well, anyway, that is how she earns her livelihood and she supported her niece as best she could.'

'As best she could, as best she could,' interrupted Rurik, looking right round the big room . . . 'Rather well, I would say. And now, are you living here?'

'Yes, Mistress Arda is happy that someone is making the most of such a lovely place.'

'And is that where you get the clothes you need?' asked the Dane, pointing to a large carved chest not far from him.

The girl blushed and lowered her head.

'Oh no,' she said, 'these clothes really are mine, and I would never want to lay a finger on Edel's things, no, never!'

'Why not?'

Mabille stayed silent, her cheeks burning, and yet she longed to talk.

For a moment the two young people felt a presence between them, Edel's presence, then the feeling evaporated and Rurik came and sat down next to Mabille.

'Did you tell Mistress Arda that I was here?' he asked.

'No, of course not, I have told no one, and I have not actually seen anyone, anyway.'

'But soon you will have to go and take refuge in the abbey, like everyone else,' retorted Rurik thoughtfully. 'Have you not been down to the village, then?'

'No I have not, only yesterday with the chevalier before you came. And as far as the tide is concerned, Drogtegand said he would come and get us, Arda and myself. The house is not as exposed as the ones down in the village. Aunt Arda told me that she has never suffered from the tides.'

'And what was it like in the village yesterday?' Rurik asked. 'Were they talking about me, looking for me?'

She stifled a nervous little laugh.

'No, sir, they had other things to think about, the procession and the tide which is on its way, and I think they've had enough of you! My cousin Landric more than anyone else, he says you could have killed him and his men but that you did not. Several villagers came back from the forest in a pitiful state. But there was someone who was happy, Drogtegand, he was rubbing his hands together with satisfaction, and I think he was smothering his laughter in that great beard of his!'

'So I do not only have enemies!' Rurik sighed.

'The chevalier is not your enemy either,' said the girl firmly.

'The chevalier? Who, pray, is the chevalier?'

'My Lord Galeran, and I think he is very nice. He is staying at the abbey, but I do not really know why he is there. He is friends with a funny little red-haired monk.'

Mabille forced herself to look closely at Rurik. The young man's face seemed to have drained of blood and his eyes were feverish.

After a while she murmured: 'But why Rurik, why did you not run away? you know you could have done. The villagers do not know the deep forest as well as you do!'

'I know, Mabille, I know only too well, but you know my people's motto: "*Nothing is ever finished until justice has been done.*" '

'You want to avenge Edel even at the risk of your own life, do you not?'

Then she added quietly: 'You still love her.'

'Did I love her?' he said with terrible sadness in his voice: 'She broke all her vows of fidelity, she broke her word and was toying with me, I raised my hand against her.'

Mabille stood up without a word. She went over to the table and started to clear up what was left of the meal in the cloth. She knew too much, but should she break her silence and betray the secrets of her only friend?

She satisfied herself with saying wearily: 'I must go and do my work now, Aunt Arda is waiting for me. Fear not, she will not come into this room, it holds too many memories for her. You are safe, no one will think that you are here. And in the end everyone will get tired of looking for you and perhaps they will find who really did the killing.'

He took her hands and looked up at her.

'Why are you doing this for me, Mabille?'

'What do you mean?'

'Why are you helping me?'

She snatched her hands away from him.

'Because I am stupid!' she said and she ran out of the room, slamming the door behind her.

40

'I am stupid,' Mabille said again, leaning back against the door that she had just closed.

Beneath her unsophisticated exterior, she hid an unusually strong will and quick mind.

'In fact,' she told herself, 'I could be protecting a murderer, because I really only have Rurik's word and it would be in his best interests, for now, to hide the truth from me. When I think about it, he is a violent man and he was certainly best placed to attack my poor Edel.

'This cannot go on for long, Rurik will have to go . . . But if he goes, if he goes . . .'

She bent her head and started to cry silently, and then the words that she did not want to speak came to her lips:

'You are like a timid rabbit, poor girl, with your head down your burrow. The real truth is that Rurik's life depends on you and on what you do.'

Mabille pulled herself together, pulled her big shawl tightly round herself and went to find Mistress Arda. As usual, the old lady was sitting embroidering by the window in her large room. Mabille touched her shoulder, and she looked up and smiled.

'Little one, I did not hear you coming. My word, you might almost think I was going deaf.'

Mabille stifled a nervous laugh. Poor woman, you are as deaf as could be, she thought.

'Tell me,' Mistress Arda went on, 'did you get some grass for the rabbits and feed the chickens?'

The girl nodded vigorously to indicate that she had.

The old woman was still smiling at her but her eyes were sad.

'You are kind, you know. I have been happy since you have been here. I know it has not been long, but I have never felt so happy. Do you see that on the table there.'

Mabille saw a package wrapped in cloth.

The old woman went on: 'I should like you to take that to the abbey straight away. If you could just give it to Tancard, the Porter, do you know him?'

'Of course, Mistress Arda, everyone knows him!' Mabille shouted.

'Go now,' continued the old woman who had not heard a thing, 'it is an offering for our patron saint, so that he may protect us during the tide.'

Mabille picked up the package, which was very light, with an uneasy smile. 'Fate has decided,' she thought.

41

The weather had deteriorated, and great dark clouds were scudding across the horizon, driven by stormy winds.

Mabille told herself she would have to travel quickly if she did not want to be soaked by the rain, and she went up the white path to the abbey almost at a run, picking her way between carts and groups of locals coming to take refuge within its fortified confines.

In the monastery the monks had a great deal to do. The Cellarer had stationed himself at the main gates and, with the help of a few villagers, was directing the new arrivals as best he could.

Apologising as she did so, Mabille slipped past people and arrived at the Porter's lodge quite out of breath. She was a little surprised not to find him standing in the doorway as he usually was, checking all the comings and goings, particularly on a day such as this.

She stopped for a moment, not quite sure what to do. Then the little door was opened and she watched a great bulky monk come out and plant himself in front of her.

'May the Lord bless you, my child!' he said, eyeing her up and down from beneath his hood. 'Can I be of help to you in any way?'

'Oh yes, Father,' said Mabille, 'This is an offering to Saint Philibert and Mistress Arda told me to give it to Tancard.'

The monk stepped back slightly and seemed to shake his head repeatedly: 'Tancard, Tancard,' he muttered, 'God rest his soul!'

Taken aback and a little frightened, Mabille whispered: 'What do you mean, Father, is he no longer of this world?'

The monk leant his head on one side:

'Just so, little one, the Lord has called him unto Him.'

'And someone gave him a lot of help!' said a clear voice behind the young girl.

Mabille turned round. The chevalier was standing before her, looking at her gravely: 'Oh yes, my dear,' he said bluntly, 'it is not just Edel. Someone has made the most of all the commotion created by the procession to sneak in here and quietly slit old Tancard's throat as if they were cutting a piglet . . . It was easy, the abbey was as good as deserted during the blessing of the river.'

Mabille had gone completely white, and she stood silently with lowered eyes.

The chevalier came over towards her and took her arm firmly.

'Now,' he said dragging her towards the track, 'I hope that you understand that this latest crime could have been avoided, if only you had confided in me the other day at the sanatorium . . . and do not go pulling any faces!' he added, seeing that she was about to cry.

She fought back her tears and murmured in a trembling voice: 'Now, now, my Lord, I am ready to tell you everything!'

42

As Rurik had the night before, the murderer hid in the thick, glossy foliage of the holly plantation.

From there he could see Mistress Arda perfectly clearly as she bent over her work at the open window.

A little earlier, in the pale light of dawn, he had glimpsed Mabille as she hurriedly picked grass for the rabbits along the edge of the track. He had moved forward several paces. Why not now? he wondered impatiently, nervously rubbing his hands up and down his hose. He had been about to throw himself onto her when, just in time, he spotted a young country boy ambling along the road driving a mule laden with faggots.

With a groan of anger, the murderer had hidden himself again. He heard Prime being rung in in the distance by the bells of the abbey, and felt suddenly indecisive. Should he go into the widow's house and snatch the little bird in her nest, or should he wait for her to come out again and kill her cleanly?

He sighed. He was anxious to be done with it and to be able, at last, to see himself rid of everything that still threatened him. Even though he was buried in his thoughts, he did not take his eyes off the dilapidated front of the big old house. Up until then, fate had played into his hands. Even old Tancard's murder had gone disconcertingly well. The old rat had looked at the beautifully sharpened blade with wide-eyed amazement. He had not even screamed when he bled him so perfectly.

'Curiosity is a nasty failing' chuckled the killer. 'The old miser was always spying on people and, on top of that, he had a tongue that never stopped wagging, so he spent his time ranting on about people. Well now he has learnt with one swift lesson how to observe the rule of silence!'

The man was still laughing as he looked slowly at his hands. It had been difficult getting them clean and shaking off the smell. The old man had emptied himself like a pig when he had bled him.

This brief lapse of attention was to prove fatal to the killer. When he looked up he saw Mabille running along the road with a package in her hand.

Disconcerted, he told himself he had time to catch up with the girl before she reached the first houses of the village. After all, the road did have thick scrub all the way along, and it would be easy to drag Mabille in and to complete his business where no one could see . . . Yes, it would be just as easy as it had been with that little harlot Edel . . .

Only, the problem was that he could hear a sort of rumbling sound in the distance. It was not yet thunder from the storm, but some wretched cart heavily laden with forage. From where he sat perched on the slats, a young boy was scolding a stubborn old horse. When he saw Mabille, his face broke into a wide smile and he said something amusing, which the killer could not hear.

The cart rolled steadily on, just a couple of paces from the holly bushes. When the assassin stood back up from behind the bushes, it was too late. The road was empty and he could no longer see Mabille who had already disappeared behind the first group of houses in the village.

Piqued, he crouched back down and stayed there a long time thinking about what to do next.

This was the first time that his plans had fallen through, he thought. He looked up at the sky, laden with dark menacing clouds. Should he wait for Mabille to come back? But he did not know how long she would be gone, it could be a long time. Yes, he had found out in the village that she was living with the widow Arda, but with the tide coming, you could not bank on anything. She might very well want to stay with her family in their little hut right next to the earth banks.

After a long while, he decided that he could put Mabille off until later and that he had other things to be getting on with. The widow was on her own and was no longer at the window. This would be a good moment. He stood up calmly, crossed the road which was at last deserted, and slipped round the side of the house. Whistling casually to himself, he went over towards the window of Edel's room.

The shutter was closed but he saw that the latch on the inside had not been pushed down.

'This really is too easy,' he groaned, regaining confidence.

He pushed the shutter back gently and went into the house.

'Actually, this is no bad thing. The widow is deaf as a post, and the other little strumpet has got it coming to her.'

After glancing round briefly and establishing that the room was empty he went impatiently over to Edel's coffer.

He pushed it, with some difficulty, towards the middle of the room and knelt down in front of it. The lock gave with a crack and he lifted the lid. He carelessly tossed aside quantities of kirtles in various colours, mantles, bonnets and petticoats . . .

At last he came to the bracelets, the precious necklaces, a pewter pitcher, silver cutlery and even a handful of finely honed hand swords.

The murderer snatched up a smaller coffer with trembling hands, and opened it. It was full of silver markas.

43

'Are you praying for the dead, you good-for-nothing? That is a doleful treasure if ever there was one!'

A voice that the murderer knew well thundered behind him. Stupefied, he turned round slowly to find that he was kneeling in front of Rurik, who had been hiding behind the curtains that surrounded the bed.

The Dane with his powerful stature towered over the wretch, and he suddenly, incongruously, burst out laughing.

'They say my people is a people of pillagers and killers, but you, you little piece of carrion, you come from quite a different race, one that walks on cloven feet and never bares its face!'

The assassin had stood up with disquieting agility and was now facing the Dane.

'What exactly are you saying and, anyway, what are you doing in Edel's room, in her bed?' he said insolently.

This was a mistake on his part because, just hearing Edel's name spoken, Rurik was overwhelmed by an uncontrollable rage. He threw himself at the smaller man with extraordinary violence, lifted him bodily off the ground, raised him up above his own head and hurled him against the wall. The man smashed into it with a sickening thud and slumped to the ground like a puppet.

The Viking was trembling with rage, he was ready to finish his victim off with a volley of punches when a piping voice froze him in his tracks.

'Come now, Rurik, the kingdom of God belongs to the gentle and meek at heart!'

The Dane looked up to see Brother Odon, old Drogtegand and the chevalier. They were outside, leaning on the window ledge as if they were watching a mummers' play. Mabille, pale as a ghost, stood behind them in the meadow.

Galeran was the first to climb through the window and go

over to the assassin, who still lay motionless on the floor. He put the ends of his fingers to the man's neck. He was still alive.

'By my faith, Rurik,' he said, nodding, 'as throws go, that was a good throw! I can tell you have worked with the harpoon.'

The young Dane, who had calmed down a little, could not help smiling.

The killer gradually regained consciousness and looked at the chevalier in amazement.

Old Drogtegand went and sat down on a settle with the solemnity of a king. The little red-haired monk settled himself modestly on a seat, and Rurik came and joined him. Mabille stayed outside.

'This looks like the end of your story, Roderic,' sighed the chevalier as he leant over Edel's betrothed. Then he turned towards Drogtegand and the Dane who were looking at him questioningly.

'At first, everything was simple, you see,' he said as if in answer to their puzzled expressions. 'Brother Odon and I had a mission. We were to investigate the state of the abbey. In fact, for some time now, His Grace Arnulphe, the Bishop of Lisieux, had been receiving complaints and alarming reports from Jumièges.

'The abbey was apparently no longer being properly governed and was sinking fast. The monks were relaxing their rules, living whatever sort of life they chose, not paying much attention to holy law. I will not dwell on those things that should remain the secrets of the church. But Brother Odon conducted this investigation masterfully *intra-muros*, if I may say so,' asserted Galeran, turning towards the monk, who did not react.

Sitting on the end of the bench, next to the tall Dane, he was obviously thinking of something else. The chevalier smiled to himself and went on.

'Only the turmoil within the abbey was not without consequence on the outside. Do you remember Bishop Gerbold who threw his Episcopal ring into the river in disgust one day? They say that this gesture of his caused a terrible epidemic of the plague, until a fisherman found the ring in the belly of a fish and brought it back to the Bishop, who then understood the terrible lesson he had been taught by our Lord.

'That is rather what has happened here, all due to the weakness of one individual whom I will not name. In this place that no one was really governing, fraternal relations gradually turned to connivance, corruption, minor misdeeds and other ills, until eventually still more abominable deeds were done.

'A corrupt young Lord, a Sexton with perverse desires, and soon poor Edel, found disembowelled in the woods near the pest-house . . .'

At these words, they heard a muffled sob. It was Rurik, his face taut and brimming with menace.

'The question that then begged an answer was simple,' continued the chevalier. 'Who was Edel really? Was she, as she seemed to be, just a scatterbrained girl who wanted to make the most of her looks and her youth? I felt straight away that her vestments were too fine for the niece of a simple embroiderer. Our Edel was far from disinterested and must have been gaining some profit from her charms. From then on, the enquiry became more complicated, she had probably entertained very many lovers, and they must be people who had the ability to pay her handsomely, more handsomely than was within the means or the taste of the local peasantry.

'I then thought again about a Sexton who robbed the dead, and of his brother, the arrogant heir to Clères who is riddled with debts . . . but mostly I thought of you, Roderic, you who purported to be Edel's intended. Were you really such a simpleton? There was something not quite right about this whole business because scum as dirty as you does not usually turn up in an abbey in deepest Normandy.

'Normally, it carries on its evil business in the darkness and stench of city back streets, where throats are cut and great swindles are played out . . . and it usually ends up on the scaffold!'

The groom managed to stand up in the face of such insults. He was obviously regaining his confidence.

'You think that little harlot Edel gained nothing from all this?'

The Dane wanted to throw himself at him, but Drogtegand held him back with a wave of his hand.

The chevalier continued implacably: 'Do you see, Roderic, in my eyes you committed your first major mistake by staying in the stables at the abbey when, because of you and your intervention at the assembly, every able-bodied man had gone off in pursuit of Rurik. What? You were going to stay there, quietly looking after the horses, you who had been so devastated and had publicly accused the Dane of Edel's murder!

'You who pretended that Edel was as pure as the driven snow, you who seemed bent on revenge! Suddenly you were quite calm and indifferent. That was when I realised that earlier, in the village square, you had been playing a part. You came onto the stage in front of the whole village: your rôle that of the simple lover, frozen with grief, and everyone thought they were witnessing a confrontation between two men who both wanted the same woman. And cleverly you kept reinforcing this idea in their minds.

'Without Mabille, in whom Edel had confided a little, I would not have been able to confirm what I had sensed for some time.'

Then the chevalier went up to the open coffer and pulled out a long cambric veil embroidered with gold thread.

'Oh, yes, the delectable Edel knew all the moves, every provocative look and languishing gaze, she knew how to roll her pretty hips . . . but, like this in my hand, she was just a delusion, a delicious piece of bait which you, the groom, used to exercise your very fruitful little trade.

'I shall say it again, yours was the oldest trade in the book and your association worked beautifully. Edel compromised noblemen, married men or monks, and all of them – willingly or not – had to come and buy your silence: you, the cuckolded intended!'

Indicating the great coffer, Galeran added, 'In here are the assets of the dead, snatched from grieving families by the Sexton . . . stolen cutlery, *markas* filched by a young nobleman from his dying father . . .'

'And what have I got to do with what that strumpet Mabille has to say? What does it prove except that Edel was a little harlot who knew how to pull the wool over everyone's eyes? The coffer belonged not to me, but to her!' spat out Edel's betrothed.

'Oh but it did, my friend, Roderic, it did have something to do with you,' said the chevalier with a fierce smile, 'because one day the lovely Edel decided to exert her talents elsewhere and to rid herself of the burden that you were to her.

'She set her heart on Rurik, got it into her head that she should marry him secretly, because she was afraid of how angry you would be, and then she could flee with her new protector, taking the booty with her.

'When you left me on the night of the revelries, it was not, as I thought, to hide your sorrow but, after Edel's provocation, to follow her and take your revenge. It was you, then, who spied on the young couple through the half-open shutter, leaving strange imprints in the mud under the wall.'

'I heard something like footsteps outside,' murmured Rurik, 'and I went out, leaving her alone . . . When I came back she was no longer there and I went to look for her.'

'Yes,' continued the chevalier, 'when Rurik came out of her house, you went in and you dragged the poor girl outside. Did you try to persuade her to stay with you, did she resist you? In any event, you killed her and, terrified of the suspicion that must inevitably fall on you, the cuckolded intended, you performed a horrible ritual.

'That way everyone would accuse the savage Viking or even the green wolf . . . you remembered that poor creature Jendeus, who had taken refuge in the abbey. To the superstitious villagers, he would become a werewolf!

'But we must get to your second inexplicable crime, the murder of your poor father, the good and upright Tancard!'

'Granted, you have always hated him and looked down on him because he was happy, as his parents were before him, with his modest responsibilities. Whereas you nourished very different ambitions, you wanted to escape from your position as a groom and now we know how you hoped to do so!

'But, more serious still, thanks to his job, your father had a keen eye and nothing passed him by. Your comings and goings, your arrogant attitude towards the Sexton and a few others eventually began to intrigue him and he kept an eye on you. He then very quickly guessed the dubious nature of your relationship with Edel, whom he considered to be a shameless hussy.

'When he heard that she was dead, he immediately thought

that you must be the culprit. He told you so, and you did not hesitate for a moment, you silenced him. Mabille, who had been poor Edel's confidante, would probably have been your next victim . . .'

So carried away were they by the chevalier's speech, that his companions barely paid any attention to the groom. Quite unexpectedly, Roderic dashed to the window and leapt fluidly over the sill. Before anyone could react, he had reached Mabille. She did her best to escape, but he grabbed her and held her to him violently. He took a knife from his boot and held the blade under Mabille's chin, then, turning to the window, he yelled: 'Don't move, any of you, or I shall cut her throat like a rabbit!'

Galeran swore, cursing his inattention. Rurik, white with anger, could not take his eyes off the couple in their hideous embrace beyond the window.

The girl was motionless, held fast by the assassin's arms. Her heart was beating so fast she felt it might burst and, sensing that it would all soon be over, she closed her eyes. This wild animal was going to bleed her as he had done Edel and Tancard.

Roderic tightened his grip, Mabille opened her mouth breathless.

The chevalier was the first to gather his wits, he went over to the window and, restraining Rurik as he did so, shouted: 'Stop it, Roderic! I will offer you a deal, man to man.'

'What would that be, my Lord?' Roderic spat back.

'I swear to you, on my honour as a knight, that I will stay here with the others until you have had time to escape. Do you hear, Roderic?'

Behind the chevalier, the Dane growled with rage.

'I hear you,' replied the groom without slackening his hold.

'With the tide coming and all the commotion there is on the peninsula, you still have a chance of escaping . . .'

'And what do I have to do in exchange?'

'You let this poor child go, she would only hold you up if you took her with you, it would only make everyone hate you the more if you hurt her! Kill her and you are a dead man, Roderic! If I do not catch you, Rurik here would make you pay for what you have done and I will not be there to stop him. And if he does not get you, then Drogtegand's men will! All those men you have toyed with for so long, all those you have pillaged and stolen from. So, what do you decide?'

The young groom stood thinking, his face dark. After a while he asked: 'Do you have your purse, my Lord?'

'Why yes.'

'Well, fill it with all the silver you can find in the coffer and toss it to me.'

Galeran did so, and threw the purse which landed at the young man's feet.

'Right, and now make the others go to the back of the room, and you, my Lord, close the shutter with the latch on the inside.'

'Let the girl go first,' said Galeran brusquely, 'then I shall close the shutter.'

'Do I have your word, my Lord?'

'You have it,' growled the chevalier, 'but do not abuse it, Roderic. My patience has its limits as does my friends'.'

The groom muttered to himself and then, with a furious shove, he pushed Mabille away. She tripped forwards and ran frantically towards the house. She climbed fumblingly over the window sill and fell into the Dane's arms; he picked her up gently and took her to sit on the settle. Mabille sighed strangely and her teeth started chattering, the room swam round her slowly. Drogtegand noticed this and, moving Rurik aside, he took hold of the girl's shoulders and made her drink a little of the medicinal brew that he kept in an aquamanile on his belt.

As he drew the shutter in, Galeran had time to see the groom snatching up the purse of silver and running towards the village.

44

The abbey's hostel was already full; the Cellarer, Onfroi, had found space there for the women, the elderly and the ailing; in all nearly sixty villagers ran in shouting and throwing their bundles down on the straw mattresses, fed their children and settled themselves down as best they could.

There were people everywhere. A few pilgrims had sneaked into the byres, sleeping in the straw next to the animals. At dawn the Abbot had arranged for lean-to shelters made of planks and tarpaulins to be built along the monastery walls as refuge for the inhabitants of Heurteauville. The whole abbey looked like a besieged village that morning.

And, as in great wars, the enemy was approaching. The great river followed its path beneath the tidal swell, and powerful waves came and smacked against the jetties and deserted pontoons. Violent gusts of wind scudded between the twin towers of Notre-Dame where the great bells continued to ring out the tocsin.

The crowd jostled in the basilica and in the church of Saint Peter to hear the Sext Mass. There was such a commotion that the monks had to force their way through the mêlée to calm the most recalcitrant of their faithful.

Abbot Eustache pulled himself up onto the stage and, standing facing the altar, he spread his arms in a sign of appeasement and prayer. At that moment, the tocsin stopped and silence fell, disturbed only by the creaking of the roof and the rain falling onto the stone paving. The bell for Sext rang out.

At the gates of Jumièges the last of the refugees were still hurrying in. On this terrible day, everyone prayed with great fervour because faith, as they often say, starts with fear . . .

45

The rain was attacking the land surprisingly violently . . . at times great cloudbursts spat down onto the peninsula, flooding the neat rows of vegetables, overflowing the fish pools, ripping branches off trees, and torrenting down the roofs of the houses and the sloping tracks. A powerful smell of sea water hung in the air. The great wave had passed Tancarville and was nearing Caudebec, sweeping filthy muddy water with it, engulfing orchards and submerging fields and woods.

Roderic was fleeing again, and was now heading for Conihout, struggling against the wind, which had the strength of a wild animal. His first instinct had been to run to the village where he could have mingled with the stragglers and made for the road to Trait and then on to Saint-Wandrille. Only, there was no one left. He sidled cautiously along the little streets flooded with slurry, but everything was deserted. He stopped to catch his breath, looking at the cottages with their tightly sealed shutters, and the planks nailed to the doors. He could not even take shelter in a house.

He jumped suddenly at the sound of voices, and hid in a corner between two buildings. Drogtegand went past with Mabille and the little red-haired monk who was helping the elderly Arda, as they made their slow and difficult progress towards the abbey.

No sign of the chevalier or the Dane. Those two must be after him already. The young man's heart missed a beat, he would have to act quickly. Neither the elder nor the chevalier were naïve. Soon all the roads would be blocked and he, Roderic, would be imprisoned on the peninsula – indeed he might be already.

A horrible sneer twisted the young man's face. 'They lied to me, I am caught like a fish in a net! And there is Rurik too,' he thought, looking around anxiously. 'That good-for-nothing wants to see me dead and he is a good hunter. There is only one solution, to go towards the river, no one will think of looking for me there.'

Roderic heard the distant echo of the bells for Sext in amongst the deafening roar of the wind and the rain. He set off at a run again, he was still a long way from the river bank when the torrents of water became very much stronger.

Everything suddenly went dark, he could no longer see a thing, even the trees closest to him disappeared behind a greyish curtain. The assassin tried to set off again but tripped on a tree stump and sprawled on the ground. The rain beat down on him remorselessly. He had never experienced a downpour like it in his life, it was as if he were swimming through turbulent waters. He got to his knees and felt his way to the base of a tree where he huddled with his arms over his head for protection. The wind and the water sliced through the leaves overhead, icily fingering the back of his neck and trickling inside his doublet. It went on like this for a long time, and then the storm gradually abated, before stopping abruptly.

Roderic looked up and coughed out water like a drowned man. He wiped his eyes clumsily with his wet sleeve, and got to his feet shakily, looking around and listening carefully.

There was no sound at all. The silence was unnatural. One of those strange, disturbing silences like a bad omen, a quiet in which people searched in vain for any little echo, even of their own footsteps. Roderic shook his head nervously and shivered.

But yes, he could hear something now . . . a distant roar he could not quite identify, like a powerful rumble of thunder booming ever closer, but it was not coming from the sky.

His eyes gaped in horror. It was the tidal wave! The tidal wave was coming, the great wall of water had passed Caudebec and was heading straight for Jumièges!

46

As the assassin had thought, after a brief discussion with Drogtegand and Odon, Galeran and Rurik had set off on his trail.

Sitting back on his heels, the young Dane had taken a bit of earth between his fingers and then had gone to look carefully over the nearby holly bushes. A few broken twigs and some bruised moss had been enough to convince him that the assassin had indeed fled towards the village. But a soft rain had started to fall and the water seeping into the ground had succeeded in erasing any traces left by the groom.

As they could find no sign of him on the outskirts of the village, Galeran had asked the young hunter to stop for a moment. The chevalier seemed perplexed: 'What would you do if you were him, Rurik?'

The young giant thought for a moment and murmured: 'I know not, my Lord. The little devil knows that we are behind him, he could try to get to Trait or to Duclair . . .'

'No, I think not. He is more cunning than that, he has probably worked out that Drogtegand's men will soon close off the peninsula. So . . .'

'So?'

'His crimes have proved it to us: he is not short on nerve or on thinking power. I am almost certain that he will try to take the only possible route, the only one left to him.'

'You mean . . . the river? But it is impossible, he is from these parts, he would know that he could not get through.'

'Not now, but tell me if I am mistaken: There is not one, but two equinox waves. If the first one is coming now, during Sext, the second one will come just about at the time of Nocturn tonight. He could of course try to get through during the night, before the second tide, but that would be too dangerous. On the other hand, shortly after Nocturn would be a more favourable time for a possible crossing.'

'Quite so, my Lord, the Seine is quieter then. It is no longer battling against the rising sea and almost goes flat. But it will still be dark and, even if he let himself be carried in a boat, the river would be full of all sorts of debris, tree trunks, animal carcasses . . .'

After a moment's thought, Rurik shook his head.

'That is not nerve, my Lord, that is madness, but it would be just as mad for him to let himself be caught again! He has no choice. You think he has gone down to the river then?'

'Yes, quite simply because he will be sure that we will not be looking for him there, and he will think that he can find some shelter there where he can wait until the tidal wave has passed. You said it yourself, Rurik, he is from these parts, he thinks he can avoid the most dangerous spots. Let us think about this, you have already spent some time here, two years, I think. Is there somewhere that you would take refuge during the great tide?'

The Dane sighed, 'You know, my Lord, the only place that is really sheltered is the higher land of the Jumièges peninsula.'

The young man paused for a moment, and then went on.

'The Terre Gémétique is a strange place. Its forests are thick, its marshes abounding with game and . . . lethal; the river is very beautiful, it is as powerful and mysterious as those in my country and it has their terrifying violence. Imagine if you can, my Lord, that everything on both banks is completely submerged when the great tide comes! And, according to Drogtegand who has seen a good many, this particular tide will be like those in old Gaitelgrime's tales. The elder has seen the signs, and I am sure that Roderic is not aware of it!'

As if to prove the young Dane right, the storm chose that moment to burst, and the rain became a deluge. The two men tried in vain to continue speaking, but could hear nothing except for the continuous hammering of water on their heads and shoulders.

Catching the chevalier by the sleeve of his tunic, Rurik dragged him towards a nearby tree. Swearing profusely, the two men untied a little boat that was fastened to its trunk, and slid beneath it to wait for the end of the squall. Once they were sheltered, the Dane took the sturdy rope and wound it carefully round himself.

To the two immobilised companions, it seemed an interminable wait and then, suddenly, the drumming of the rain on the hull stopped dead.

47

The north wind was venting its full fury on the land, violent squalls tore sections of the cottage roofs away despite the fishing nets, and broke off great branches which it hurled about as it went.

Soaked to the skin, Roderic shivered with cold or with fear, he was not sure which. But what he did feel was that his time was nearly up. He had learnt as a child that the tidal wave could be heard thundering when it was still two leagues away, and that it travelled with the speed of a galloping horse!

He had to move at whatever cost. He clung to the least bump in the ground, leaning against the wind and finally coming close to his goal. Before him were the outlines of the first houses of Conihout where he wanted to take refuge. He knew that no one would come looking for him there. It was too dangerous.

He remembered, because he had taken part in its construction, that since the last work had been done under Drogtegand's instructions, a protective tide barrier had been built there and that the town, like Heuteauville on the opposite bank, was not as vulnerable to the tides as it used to be. Of course, the ground was already under water, and the fields and houses flooded, but there was one house that he knew, a storage barn built by the abbey, that was made of stone and was taller than the others, and the tide never reached its attics. He knew that he could wait there for the best moment to cross the river and to escape those who were out for his skin.

The river waters in front of him were cleaving in two, announcing the arrival of the great wave, and then, quite suddenly, he saw it and he opened his eyes wide with terror.

He had never seen one like it! It must have been at least 40 feet high. It rose up between the cliffs like a black wall, taller than the enclosure of the abbey, a wall that was hurtling towards him!

Terrified and with his blood beating in his temples, Roderic looked around, dazed with fear. The immense body of water had already passed Yainville, it would be upon him in just a few moments. It was then that he saw them on the fringes of the wood.

Rurik and Galeran, both out of breath, had seen Roderic too, and they had seen the advancing wave at the same moment.

'What should we do, my Lord?' breathed the Dane. 'If we carry on, we are dead!'

The chevalier considered their options in a flash. The assassin was before them but Galeran could see only too well the ominous silhouette of the wave advancing behind him. Even in his own region, he had never seen one so tall.

Cupping his hands round his mouth, in an effort to be heard despite the wind, he bellowed at the top of his voice: 'Roderic, come back! Come back!'

The chevalier was about to set off towards him, but the Dane held him back.

'He cannot hear you, my Lord, we must get out! That wave is not like any other I have seen.'

The Dane was already looking around, trying to find some idea to save them both.

Roderic was still hesitating, he saw the wave hurling itself onto the peninsula with a great roar. The two men were shouting something he could not hear.

He bent into the wind and set off again towards the store house. A ladder fixed to the dry stone façade meant that he could climb swiftly up to the attic.

From where he stood, Galeran saw Roderic slip through a gap in the roof. Rurik was already tugging his sleeve: 'Quickly, quickly, come chevalier, over there, the alder trees!'

In the eerie yellowish light around them, the chevalier could make out the contours of a copse, and towering above it the great boughs of several ancient trees. In a flash, he grasped the Dane's idea, and sped off in his wake with his head down.

They were now enveloped by the humid breath of the wave with its smell of marine disintegration, a smell which for once evoked nothing other than a fresh tomb. As he ran towards the little wood, the Dane loosened the thick rope that he had wound round his chest. With the chevalier on his heels, he stopped at the foot of the tree he had singled out, an old alder with massive branches.

Without really knowing how, they climbed the tree and perched up in the main branches.

Rurik threw one end of the rope to the chevalier and the two men wound it swiftly round the great trunk before slipping themselves between the loops of rope.

Hauling it in, they tightened the rope around themselves until they were pressed hard up against the bark. Then the Dane deftly knotted the heavy hemp with a series of strong sailor's knots.

Behind them, the wave was already engulfing the banks of the river, snapping the pontoons, carrying away sections of flood barrier ten-foot high as if they were wisps of straw, hurling itself onto the houses of Conihout, which were instantly submerged, tearing up the cottage roofs, crashing through the cob walls . . .

The two men felt the old tree creaking. They pressed themselves against the trunk, holding the ropes tightly in their fists. They exchanged a brief look, and the chevalier said gravely: 'May God keep us, Rurik. You are a valiant companion, such as any man would wish to have with him at such a moment!'

The Dane nodded.

'May He have pity on us, my Lord!'

The two men could not say anything else. The tide was upon them. They stiffened, instinctively closing their eyes and taking great lungfuls of air as if they were about to dive. The wave passed over above the top of the huge tree, covering it with silt and striking it such a mighty blow that the men felt it quake in its foundations before they were submerged and lost consciousness.

48

When the chevalier regained consciousness, he was still attached to the tree trunk and had no clear idea of where he was. He felt that every bone in his body had been broken, as he did when he came out of battle.

He turned his head slowly and opened his eyes. He was covered in silt, and blood and salt water streamed from his mouth.

An apocalyptic silence hovered over the peninsula.

He looked beside him and breathed a sigh of relief. Rurik was still there, slumped in the restraining ropes. His face was covered in bruises, but his chest rose and fell regularly.

'Rurik! Are you all right?' Galeran murmured, nudging him.

The other man opened his eyes, looked at the chevalier and gave a deep laugh.

'Well, we have come back from the brink, as they say, but in what a state!'

The chevalier smiled and nodded.

'Quite so, we have come back from the brink.'

As the Dane had predicted, the woodland around them had withstood the wave fairly well, protecting them from the full force of the waters. But beyond there was nothing left but a desolate expanse, dotted with debris which was sinking slowly into a cloying, greyish slurry . . .

The chevalier took up his dagger and cut the ropes that had held them fast. Then he looked up. The great tree had lost all its leaves as if it were dead. Galeran placed his palms against the silted surface of the wood and, with a smile playing on the corners of his lips, he silently thanked the spirit of the black tree, the alder, the tree of the dead waters, for having saved them.

The two men slipped cautiously back down to the ground and the chevalier groaned.

'We will have to go and see whether we are the only ones to have survived.'

'Oh, yes indeed, Roderic!' grumbled Rurik.

The two men made their way round the tall trees and, as they looked over towards the river bank and the hamlet of Conihout, they stopped in their tracks, dumbfounded.

'But, but . . .' stammered the Dane.

'There is nothing left, Rurik, nothing at all.'

Before them stretched out a great expanse covered in muddy water, here and there a tree trunk emerged, a ruined wall, a broken boat . . .

Forging their way through with the aid of sticks for balance, the two men moved steadily closer. The water came half-way up their hose. What had been pasture was still flooded and just a few paces from them the river was rushing towards a canal that it had carved out for itself, heading straight for the middle of what had once been Conihout.

'Our dear groom would have done better to have taken refuge somewhere else. He has settled his debts!' said the chevalier darkly, indicating the place where the store house had stood, where nothing but part of one crumpled wall remained.

The wind had dropped.

The two men contemplated the vast expanse before them, glimmering like a film of black silver. A little further on, a huge crevasse was swirling furiously with fetid black sludge.

'What, pray, is that?' asked the chevalier.

'The Haugues' hole, my Lord. When the tides are especially high, the water goes in there and comes back out like that. The gap gets larger every year.'

'It is like in my home country, around Arez,' murmured the chevalier. 'We called it the Yehun, the mouth of hell! It is the internal sea which, every once in a while, wells up above the earth!'

49

The night had passed and a new dawn had risen over the Terre Gémétique. After the equinoctial storm and the terrible days that went with it, the sky was clear once again and the stars seemed just an arm's reach away.

The heat of the last few days of September had dried out the strands, and the sludge that had smothered them blew away in a fine grey dust that smelled of salt and the depths of the sea. The river still towed pieces of debris and broken tree-trunks, making it dangerous to navigate between the two devastated banks.

Rurik and Mabille had decided to take a walk along the Seine. Rurik had taken Mabille's hand, and this simple contact had moved him more profoundly than any embrace he had so far known.

He heaved a strange sigh and glanced anxiously at the girl walking beside him.

'Oh dear, Mabille,' he said numbly, 'there is so much that I want to tell you. That is why I wanted to meet you this evening.'

She tilted her head up and looked him squarely in the eye.

I have never been looked at with such simplicity, such sincerity, he thought.

'I cannot stay here after everything that has happened,' Rurik murmured. 'The locals have rejected me, they wanted me dead. Even if they now repent of their injustice, I have to leave.'

The girl bent her head to one side and lowered her eyes, and they walked on in silence for a long while.

'Mabille, do you know why Edel wanted to be my wife?' Rurik asked suddenly.

The young girl hesitated for a moment before murmuring, 'Because she loved you.'

'Is that what she told you?'

The girl's cheeks flushed scarlet and she gave no reply.

'Come now, you do not answer so readily now because you

know full well that she loved only herself,' he said sadly. 'It just so happens that some months before the terrible night on which we were married – and on which I was to learn so many hideous truths – I received a message and some important news.

'My older brother, Rollon, who served under the orders of Jocelin II of Courtenay, was killed while the Atabeg Zengi were capturing Edesse. That made me the inheritor of my family's lineage; I was no longer just a younger brother with no inheritance of his own. My family has close blood ties with the Giroie clan. So Edel was not hoping to marry an impoverished exile but the only son of a Danish lord.'

'That was her great dream of the Orient, then,' said Mabille almost in a whisper, 'that is why she wanted to leave her intended.'

They were now near the jetty where fishermen were casting little nets with lead weights, by the light of their torches.

'Look, are the reflections in the water not pretty,' murmured Mabille, 'they look like thousands of stars.'

They were both thinking the same thing. Now, our hands will part and we will be separated for ever. We will never see each other again, and it will be too late.

The young girl turned resolutely to Rurik and said: 'Kiss me!'

The Dane stepped back slightly. An old fisherman who had been watching the couple for a while called out.

'Well, my boy, if a pretty girl like that had said as much to me, I would not be standing back, I can tell you.'

They started to laugh. Rurik took Mabille by the hand and led her a little distance away, to the shelter of the great alder trees. There he took her in his arms, gently as if she were fragile, and their lips met for the first time, awkwardly like two bashful children.

50

Brother Odon was sitting on the chevalier's straw mattress, watching his friend gathering up his tack, and tidying his cell.

'So, you are going then,' he said sadly, 'and I too must soon leave.'

The chevalier turned his piercing blue eyes to the diminutive monk.

'Fie, Odon, you know as well as I do that we will see each other again some day. We make a very good team!'

'You say that but . . .' murmured Odon, casting his eyes to the skies. 'You said you were going back to your family "at the ends of the earth", but I know that you will actually be joining someone quite different there.'

Taken aback, Galeran turned to face Odon.

'You are doing it again, my friend, playing the soothsayer! You seem to know wither I go better than I do.'

'Yes,' said Odon teasingly, 'as it happens I can see a wide shore and the sea where seals are at play. There is also an abandoned chapel, and in the distance I can see a woman on horseback, spurring on her steed . . . As for what follows,' said Odon, modestly lowering his eyes, 'I will say no more . . . But remember the dangers of the flesh, my friend!'

Galeran smiled. 'Oh Odon! Odon! You will never know how much those dangers—'

'No, thank you,' said the monk a little curtly. 'While we are on the subject, do you know who was wed last night and managed, once again, to give the old priest of Jumièges the fright of his life by breaking into the church?'

'How would I know, being so short-sighted?'

'Well, it was Rurik.'

'So, he had another go!'

'Why yes! It was with little Mabille this time.'

'And how exactly do you know this?' asked Galeran who was beginning to feel a little put out.

'Because this morning, at first light, they came to find me and I blessed them before they left.'

'I see, so they have already left?'

'Quite so, Mabille told me that they were going far, far away, to Rurik's family.'

'And where would that be?'

'In the Orient.'

The chevalier looked quite dazed and said falteringly:

'The Orient! Her too. Are these girls all quite mad, then?'

'Probably, very probably,' said Odon, looking pensively at the floor. 'You know, Galeran, celibacy has its merits. You should consider it. For my part, I bless our Lord every day for not having taken a wife!'

'May this be the end of the book
But not the end of the journey.'

Bernard de Clairvaux

Author's note

Since the tumultuous month of September 1145, more than eight hundred and fifty years have passed over the Terre Gémétique and the Abbey of Jumièges.

From the cliffs opposite, its tall white towers can still be seen emerging from the surrounding forest. The ferry crosses steadily over the waters of the great river to this day, even though it is no longer hauled on ropes. And, although they no longer swim upstream along the Seine, seals and whales are still seen off the coast of Normandy.

Mediaeval Recipes
From the Time of the
Chevalier de Lesneven

Honeyed capon pâté

4 breasts of capon or chicken
2 eggs, separated
150g butter
salt
light white wine (optional)
100g of unsalted pistachio nuts
3 tablespoons of acacia honey
100g of currants
(marinated overnight in a little red wine)
Bread dough
(or flaky pastry)

This pâté, which is very similar to the celebrated petits pâtés de Pézenas, combines the full flavour of poultry with the delicate aroma of honey and pistachio nuts.

- Finely chop the capon breasts and the pistachio nuts.
- Blend them with the butter, egg yolks, salt and acacia honey.
- Add the currants (if the mixture is too dry, moisten with a little light white wine).
- Spread a thin layer of bread dough (or flaky pastry) in a buttered pie dish.
- Cover it with the pâté mixture and seal with another layer of dough.
- Cook in a moderate oven.

Crème d'or

This creamy delight owes its pretty name to the saffron used to flavour it. Like most mediaeval desserts, it is based on an almond 'milk' which must be prepared the day before.

    120g unpeeled sweet almonds
    50g of rice starch
    5 or 6 pistils of saffron
    5 cloves
    1 cinnamon stick
    salt
    1 tablespoon of mixed flower honey
    (or, preferably, acacia honey)
    50g of pine kernels or flaked almonds

- Prepare the almond 'milk' the day before by steeping the whole almonds in a little fresh water. The currants should be soaked overnight too.
- To skin the almonds, simply throw them into boiling water, drain them and then run them under cold water. The brown skin then slips off easily if the almonds are pinched between the thumb and forefinger.
- Take the skinned almonds and blend them until smooth in a litre of fresh water.
- Thicken this almond 'milk' with the rice starch.
- Bring the mixture to the boil slowly, stirring all the time. The mixture should have a creamy consistency.
- Remove from the heat and add the cinnamon stick, cloves, currants, salt and honey, and the saffron which gives it a beautiful golden yellow colour.
- Cover and leave to infuse for 15 minutes.
- Remove the cinnamon stick and cloves.
- Stir the fragrant mixture and pour it into small individual dishes.
- Leave to chill for a few hours.
- Sprinkle with grilled pine kernels or flaked almonds, and add a pinch of ground cinnamon.

This golden cream is delightful with a glass of fine dessert wine.

Oriental rose honey

This recipe, brought back from the Orient in the times of the Crusades, should be prepared the day before.

125g of acacia honey
100g of very fragrant red rose petals

- Put the honey in a small pan and bring to the boil slowly.
- As soon as foam appears on the surface, remove it from the heat and toss the rose petals into the honey.
- Leave to infuse overnight.
- The following day bring to the boil again, and remove from the heat immediately.
- Strain the honey but leave one or two fragrant petals floating in the golden liquid.
- Put the honey in pots, seal them and turn them upside down.
- Leave to cool upside down.

Eau de fraises des bois

In the Middle Ages, people rarely drank pure water, they preferred to flavour it with fruit juices or spices. To make one litre you will need:

1 litre of fresh water
1kg of wild strawberries or very fragrant cultivated strawberries
(choose very ripe ones, clean them and hull them)
A few leaves of fresh mint
300g of acacia honey
(or 400g of sugar if preferred)
250ml of sweet white wine, such as Grenache

- Bring the water and the honey to the boil in a pan and boil for five minutes.
- Remove from the heat and put in the strawberries.
- Cover and leave to infuse for at least two hours.

- Sieve the mixture taking care not to crush the fruit through.
- Add the wine and put into bottles.
- Chill for at least four hours.
- Put a few fresh mint leaves into each glass before serving.

Bon appétit!

Glossary

Aquamanile a water carrier made from a pig or sheep's bladder or from a gourd

Bailiff a feudal lord's overseer, usually his closest, most trusted servant

Ballock dagger a small dagger with two small balls (ballockys) at the end of the handle to stop the user's hand slipping onto the blade

Besom broom a broom made of twigs in the shape of a 'witch's broom'

Capuchon a hooded cape

Chapter a meeting of the members of a monastic order

Chasuble a long-sleeved overgarment worn by priests during Mass

Childer, childling colloquial terms for young children

Cot a common mediaeval word for a simple bed which may have constituted just a straw mattress, or may have had a simple wooden frame

Cottars peasant workers on a large estate, having less standing than villeins (see p. 226)

Dorter a dormitory for several people in a monastery or convent

Doublet a fitted waist- or hip-length tunic usually made of wool, worn by men throughout the Middle Ages

Frater the dining-room or refectory in a monastery or convent

Head-wrap a simple white linen bonnet

Hvalt whale in Danish

Kirtle a dress of linen or wool

Lavatorium an area in a monastery or convent used for washing

Mantle a coat or cape, often of wool or leather

Markas silver or gold measure (= 245 grammes)

Mesne the parts of an estate that were worked by tenant farmers or villeins

Mummers performers, usually masked

Oblation a person given by their family in offering to a monastery

Palfrey a light riding horse

Peona gravissima capital punishment

Pest-house a single house or small community set apart from towns and villages where the sick, especially lepers, were tended to

Quillon a small sharp sword

Rebec a stringed instrument, a forebear of the modern violin

Scriptorium a place where books and documents were stored and copied

Sedilia the throne-like seat of the highest officiator during Mass and a variety of meetings

Shift a white linen undershirt

Surcoat an outer garment made of wool or leather, sometimes with fur trimmings

Tabula plicata a folding table

Vellum fine parchment made from calf- or pig-skin

Villeins serfs who swore fealty to the local lord. He would allocate them a plot of land to work and they would pay him with their crops and/or livestock

Vivarium a place where live animals were kept and bred to supply the kitchens of a large establishment

Wax tablet and stylus a tablet of wood coated in wax and a sharp instrument made of wood, bone or metal were used throughout the Middle Ages, especially for communication between monks observing the rule of silence

The mediaeval monastic timetable

Nocturn: Mass held towards 2 o'clock in the morning
Matins: Mass held just before dawn
Prime: Mass held at about 7 o'clock in the morning
Terce: Mass held at about 9 o'clock in the morning
Morrow Mass: held in the middle of the morning

Sext: the sixth Mass of the day, held at midday

None: Mass held at 2 o'clock in the afternoon

Vespers: from the Latin word vespera, evening. Mass held at about 5 o'clock in the afternoon

Compline: Mass held at about 8 o'clock in the evening.

Prominent figures
in the 12th century

Eleanor of Aquitaine: (1122 – 1204) After her divorce from Louis VII in 1152 she married Henry Plantagenet in the same year and bore him several children (most notably Richard the Lionheart). She ended her days in the Abbey at Fontevrault where she is buried.

Louis VII: (1120 – 1180) King of France, crowned in Reims on 25 October 1131. In 1137 he married Eleanor of Aquitaine. He participated in the second crusade with Conrad III. He was divorced in 1152 and married Constance de Castille. After her death, he married Adèle de Champagne, mother of Philippe II Auguste. He died on 18 September 1180.

Suger: (1081 – 1151) Monk and politician. He became Abbot of Saint-Denis in 1122 and was a friend and fellow student of Louis VI. He acted as an advisor to Louis VII and was Regent to the Kingdom of France during the second crusade.

Abelard: (1070 – 1142) Philosopher, theologian and dialectician. He founded the Abbey of Paraclet where Eloise became Abbess. Bernard de Clairvaux obtained his condemnation at the Council of Sens in 1140.

Bernard de Clairvaux: (1091 – 1153) Having taken holy orders in Cîteaux in 1112, he became the first Abbot of Clairvaux in 1115. In Vézelay in 1146 he was a great advocate of the second crusade. He argued against the *Ordre de Cluny*.

Roger II of Sicily: From the Norman Hauteville dynasty, died in Palermo in 1154.

Honorius d'Autun: (or Augustodunensis) attributed with authorship of *De imagine mundi*, a panoramic encyclopaedia of the world of the 12th century.

Maud or Matilda, the 'Empress Maud': (1102 – 1167) Daughter of Henry I of England. Married the German Emperor, Henry V (1114), then Geoffrey V, Count of Anjou (1128). She was the legitimate heir to the English throne, but it was seized by Stephen of Blois against whom she conducted a civil war.

Stephen of Blois: King of England from 1135 to 1154. He usurped the throne that should have gone to 'Empress Maud', but, on the death of his son in 1153, he appointed as his successor Maud's son, Henry Plantagenet, the husband of Eleanor of Aquitaine.

Arnulphe, Bishop of Lisieux: A man of letters much respected by Bernard de Clairvaux, he governed Lisieux for forty years and left many great works. He was a great negotiator and acted as the legate of Pope Eugene III during the second crusade.

Abbot of Eustache of Jumièges: Abbot from September 1142 until his death in December 1154.

Abbot Guillaume II: Abbot of Jumièges from 1128 until his death on 10 August 1142.